Life And Love Continue

Life and Love Continue
Copyright © 2024 by Judith Cottingham Perkins

Published in the United States of America

Library of Congress Control Number: 2024909339
ISBN   Paperback: 979-8-89091-621-1
ISBN   eBook: 979-8-89091-622-8

All rights reserved. No part of this publication may be reproduced, stored in a retrieval system or transmitted in any way by any means, electronic, mechanical, photocopy, recording or otherwise without the prior permission of the author except as provided by USA copyright law.

The opinions expressed by the author are not necessarily those of ReadersMagnet, LLC.

ReadersMagnet, LLC 10620 Treena Street, Suite 230 | San Diego, California, 92131 USA

1.619. 354. 2643 | www.readersmagnet.com

Book design copyright © 2024 by ReadersMagnet, LLC. All rights reserved.

Cover design by Ericka Obando
Interior design by Kristiana Badayos

Life And Love Continue

THE MEMORIES OF

Judith Cottingham Perkins

Dedication

To my Grandchildren, Great-Grandchildren and those that follow, may you always know where you come from and that you are loved and cherished beyond measure. This book was written for you.

Grandma Judy

CONTENTS

Introduction xi
Glossary Of Nicknames xiii

Chapter 1:   Pa and his Chums 1
Chapter 2:   Mary Bowman Brunner (Bumma) 3
Chapter 3:   Alice Blanche Stuart (Nano) 5
Chapter 4:   Voyle Brunner and Margaret Simmons 8
Chapter 5:   The Young Mary Alice 10
Chapter 6:   Tom Cottingham and Mary Alice Brunner 12
                "Doctor vs. Doctor" 16
                "Be Kind to Jimmy Day" 17
Chapter 7:   Margaret Brunner (Nanama) 19
                "Fudge and Divinity" 21
                "Canning and Jelly Making" 21
Chapter 8:   What we know of Tom and his Family 24
Chapter 9:   Estella Mitchell Cottingham (Mom) 28
Chapter 10: 4306 S. E. Ramona 31
                "Margarine and Friends" 34
                "Telephones and Party Lines" 35
                "Pinochle and Bedtimes" 35
                "Bedtime" 36
                Car vs. Table 36
                "Broken Glass" 37
                "The Dreaded Piano Lessons" 38
Chapter 11: Jo 40
Chapter 12: Portland's Union Station (The Depot) 41
Chapter 13: Living with Grandparents 43
Chapter 14: Vacations with Mama and Daddy 49

    Cannon Beach 49
    "Grapeview on Puget Sound"................................50
Chapter 15: From Danny to Dan 53
    "Pumpkin Pie"..55
Chapter 16: Voyle Oliver Brunner (Buppa)................................57
Chapter 17: The House at 3369 S. E. Schiller.............................60
Chapter 18: The Courtship of John Talbott And Mary
    Alice Cottingham..63
Chapter 19: Life after High School 66
Chapter 20: Aunt Dede 72
Chapter 21: The Old Stuart Hotel..74
Chapter 22: Driving to Alaska 76
Chapter 23: Judy's Adventures in Europe...................................79
Chapter 24: Bus trip to New Jersey...85
Chapter 25: The Meeting, Courtship and Marriage of
    Alan Perkins and Judy Cottingham 88
Chapter 26: Life with a Traveling Salesman................................97
Chapter 27: The Joys Of Moving..99
Chapter 28: The House on North 29th.....................................103
Chapter 29: The Red House 108
Chapter 30: Feeding Three Growing Boys Or The
    Dreaded Brown Pan 113
Chapter 31: Pat and Jo-Elle..114
Chapter 32: The Weddings of Jeffrey and Jennifer 117
Chapter 33: Singapore 119
Chapter 34: Traveling by Motorhome after Retirement.............123
Chapter 35: Nine Year Trips...128
Chapter 36: Short Trips 133
    Washington..133
    Oregon 135
Chapter 37: Yuma in the Winter Or Being Snowbirds 137
Chapter 38: Jill 139
Chapter 39: Being Grandparents..141
Chapter 40: Weddings 142
Epilogue..143
Acknowledgements...147

COVER PHOTO

The cover photo is of the Stuart Hotel in Riperia, Washington, circa 1908. My Great-Great Grandfather, William Henry Stuart and his wife, Mary Jane Stuart owned the hotel and raised their family there. The hotel was demolished and the town was partially flooded with the creation of the pool behind the Lower Monument Dam on the Snake River. Riperia is quiet now, the only sounds are those of the flies and the fish jumping to catch them.

The original photo and negative are owned by Patrick Perkins, the son of the Author.

INTRODUCTION

One day I was thinking about a story my mother told me years ago about her grandfather. He was called "Pa" and he called his grandchildren his "Chums". It dawned on me that there was no one else in the family who knew that story. I am the last of my generation.

When I was born, I had a great-great grandmother, two great-grandmothers, two grandmothers, a grandfather, a mother, a father, and a brother. I was two when my great-great grandmother died, ten when one great-grandmother died, twenty when the other great-grandmother died, fifteen when both my grandfather and father died, sixteen when one grandmother died and twenty when the other grandmother died. I was forty-four when my brother died and sixty when my mother died. I had the privilege of knowing all but my great-great grandmother well, and I loved listening to the tales they would tell about family, friends, and their activities when they were young.

I turned 80 last year, and realized that if I did not write some of these stories down, they would be lost.

I have included some recent events in this missive. I have had the opportunity to experience so much in my 80 years. My main purpose in writing this is so that my children, grandchildren, and those that follow will know about their ancestors and know a little about their heritage.

To my family, please know that these are my memories. They might differ from yours. I have tried to be as accurate as possible and relay what a special and diverse family we are.

In writing this, I have remembered so much about my life. One memory triggered another. I have gained an even greater appreciation for those who shared with me, took care of me, and loved me. So many good memories and fun times come to mind, and I do miss the ones who are gone.

Life and Love Continue.

GLOSSARY OF NICKNAMES

Name	Nickname	Relationship
Danton Oliver Brunner	Pa	Great-Grandfather
Mary Clair Bowman Brunner	Bumma	Great-Grandmother
Alice Blanche Stuart Simmons Wineland	Nano	Great-Grandmother
Henry IO Stuart	Uncle IO	Great-Great Uncle
Stella Stuart Dobkins	Aunt Stella	Great-Great Aunt
Winnefred Stuart Hobson	Aunt Minnie	Great-Great Aunt
Laura Valeda Stuart Berry	Aunt Dede	Great-Great Aunt
Voyle Oliver Brunner	Buppa	Grandfather
Margaret Irene Simmons Brunner	Nanama	Grandmother
Winnefred Simmons Bright	Aunt Polly	Great Aunt
Henry Simmons	Uncle Hank	Great Uncle
Estella Mitchell Cottingham	Mom	Grandmother
Mary Alice Brunner Cottingham Talbott	Mama	Mother
Thomas A. Cottingham	Daddy	Father
Danton Thomas Cottingham	Danny/Dan	Brother

CHAPTER I
Pa and his Chums

Danton Oliver Brunner was born in Ohio in 1849. He married Mary Clair Bowman and together they raised 4 children: Voyle, Earl, Faye, and Karl. He immigrated with his family to Spokane, WA and then to Portland, Oregon.

Little is known of their young life except that Pa had one eye missing due to an accident when he was a child and Mary was totally blind. They raised their family with all the challenges a sighted family would have had in the late 19th Century. In later years, they lived with their daughter Faye, her husband Roy and grandson Joe in Southeast Portland.

Danton and Mary's son Voyle and his wife, Margaret and daughter Mary Alice lived in Canby, Oregon and would pack up their Model T Ford and venture into Portland to visit. Canby was 28 miles South of Portland and a ½ day trip. They would stay for 2 days and then make the long drive home. Voyle's days off were Monday and Tuesday, so they would have to wait for school holidays to make the trip into town.

Pa was an attorney and worked in a law firm in downtown Portland. He would take the trolley from 39th and S. E. Holgate, across the Morrison Street Bridge to his office. When it was time to come home, he would reverse the route, but when he got off the trolley, his Grandchildren, Mary Alice, and Joe would be there to greet him and walk home with him.

Pa called his grandchildren his "Chums" and would avidly listen to their tales about school and their activities. He always had a piece of candy for them in his suit coat pockets.

The time would go by quickly and soon it was time to pack up and return home to Canby, only to wait for the next time they could visit.

Both Joe and Mary Alice adored their "Pa" and had very fond memories of him. Pa died November 16, 1933. He was 84 years old.

Love Continues.

CHAPTER 2

Mary Bowman Brunner (Bumma)

Mary Alice Brunner - 90 years old

Mary Brunner was my great-grandmother. She was married to Danton Oliver Brunner and her nickname was Bumma.

Bumma was blind. She could only see the color red. She raised her family performing all the chores a mother and homemaker would do in the late 1800's. She moved to Spokane, WA, then eventually to Portland, Oregon.

Bumma and Pa lived with their daughter, Faye, her husband Roy and their son Joe. Her birthday was on January 1, so we spent New Year's Day at Auntie Faye's house celebrating Bumma's birthday. The men would be in another room listening to the football game, the ladies would be in the kitchen fixing dinner and I would sit with Bumma in the living room. I would lay my head on her lap, and she would pet my hair. Her hands were so soft, and it would feel so good. She would not talk much, but she would giggle. She was always happy when her family was around.

Mama would dress me in red with a red bow in my hair. That way, Bumma could see me. Bumma died in March 1952 at the age of 99. I have such fond memories of the time I spent with her and feel so fortunate to remember her.

The Love of Family Continues.

CHAPTER 3
Alice Blanche Stuart (Nano)

Alice, the oldest daughter of William and Mary Stuart was born in Portland, Oregon in 1879. The family soon moved to Riperia, WA, a small town in Eastern Washington along the Snake River where William and Mary had purchased the hotel. Alice eventually had three sisters, Stella, Minnie, and Laura and one brother, Henry IO.

Alice, her three sisters, and one brother all worked in the hotel. It was the largest building in the town and housed the post office, bank, restaurant and lounge and the mayor's office.

The Stuart girls waited tables, cleaned the hotel, and generally kept the place neat and tidy. As they grew, they also made themselves available to the railroad workers who stayed there.

Riperia was at the end of the railway line where the trains switched engines and reversed their route, heading West along the Snake and Columbia Rivers.

Alice met and eventually married Lawyer Eugene Simmons on March 13, 1894. Their daughter Margaret was born on March 14, 1894. It Is said that William took a shotgun to the wedding. Margaret had two siblings, Winnifred, and Henry. The family lived in several cities in Southwest Washington, but finally settled in Riperia. Not much is known about the early childhood of the three Simmons children. Records show that they all went to school in Riperia. Margaret and Henry both continued their education after high school. Winnifred met and married Dana Bright and moved to Reno, Nevada. They had one child, Dana Jr.

Henry married Betty Macalar and had two children, Betty Gene and Douglas. They settled in Salem, Oregon.

Margaret met and married Voyle O. Brunner and had Mary Alice. Both Alice and Lawyer worked in the hotel. Lawyer was also the postmaster for a time. He died in 1905.

Alice continued to work, mainly on a tugboat going up and down the Snake and Columbia Rivers. They went as far as Celilo Falls on the Columbia, then back again. They would ferry workers down the river to The Dalles, Oregon. Often the Palouse Indians would ride along. Celilo Falls was a favored fishing site for them, especially when the Salmon were migrating. Nano would cook for the Indians and in turn they would give her little trinkets to say thank you. She had a lot of beautiful arrow heads and different kinds of rocks. When she lived with Uncle IO, she had a trunk full of mementos. As she was telling a story, she would open the trunk and show me some of the trinkets that she had.

LIFE AND LOVE CONTINUE

Nano never owned her own home. She always lived with a relative. When Voyle and Margaret bought their home in Portland, she decided to live with them. She was there until 1939 when Uncle IO's wife died, and he needed her help. She lived with her brother until her death.

Nanama and Buppa would often take me with them when they visited Nano and Uncle IO. I would sit and listen to her talk about Riperia and Eastern Washington and love every bit of it.

In 1908, after Lawyer Simmons death, Nano married Jack Wineland. Jack served in the Army during World War I with General Pershing. Unfortunately, the marriage did not last, and they were divorced when he returned home from the war.

Nano died on May 22, 1962. I still miss her and her stories.

But life does continue.

CHAPTER 4

Voyle Brunner and Margaret Simmons

Voyle O. Brunner   Margaret Simmons

Margaret Irene Simmons was born in Dayton, WA on March 14, 1894. Soon after her birth, the family moved back to Riperia, WA. She went to school there and continued her schooling at Lewis Clark Normal School in Lewiston, ID. She studied home economics with an emphasis on cooking.

Voyle Oliver Brunner was born in Somerset, Ohio on April 12, 1885. He moved to Spokane, WA when he was 16, and had many jobs before going to work for the railroad. He traveled all over the Northwest and Southwest United States and worked for several different railroad companies.

Voyle went to work for the Camas Prairie Railroad and the last stop on the line was Riperia. He would take his meals at the Stuart Hotel and that is where he met Margaret. Little is known about their early life together, except that they had one daughter, Mary Alice.

And life does indeed continue.

The Depot at Riperia

CHAPTER 5

The Young Mary Alice

Voyle and Mary Alice

Mary Alice Brunner was born on March 6, 1915 to Voyle and Margaret Brunner. She was to be their only child. Voyle worked for the railroad and by the nature of his job, moved around a lot. When Mary Alice was 2, they moved from Riperia, Washington to Umatilla, Oregon, then to Glendale, Oregon.

The family moved to several other cities in the Willamette Valley before settling for a while in Canby, Oregon. Mary Alice went to school in Canby from the 5th grade to the 10th grade. After 5 years in Canby, they transferred to Mill City, Oregon where Mary Alice

LIFE AND LOVE CONTINUE

graduated from Mill City High School in 1933. After graduation, she went to Oregon Normal School in Monmouth, OR.

As with everything else, the Depression hit the railroad industry very hard, and Voyle lost his job in Mill City. They were determined that Mary Alice was going to school and had saved her tuition money for the 2 years it would take to get her teaching certificate.

At that time, Voyle's job included taking the telegrams off the wire and delivering them to the proper person. When the notice came that the banks were going to close, Voyle went to the bank, withdrew the $100.00 he had saved and then went back, got the telegram, and delivered it to the bank manager. He always said that not delivering that wire in a timely manner was the only truly dishonest thing that he had ever done.

Because Voyle had lost his job, he and Margaret put their belongings into storage and traveled up and down the Willamette Valley working at whatever railroad jobs were available. During the breaks from school, Mary Alice would join them. When she was in school, she received mail from them, and every envelope had a picture drawn on the face of the envelope. Many times, the picture indicated what was written inside the envelope.

In 1935, she graduated from Normal School and obtained her teaching certificate. She was offered a job in Glendale, Oregon.

By chance a young man that Mary Alice went to school with also had a job in Glendale. Tom Cottingham had received his teaching certificate and had a job in the same school. They started dating, became engaged and got married on July 31, 1937.

With Love, Life Continues.

CHAPTER 6

Tom Cottingham and Mary Alice Brunner

Tom and Mary Alice

Tom Cottingham and Mary Alice Brunner met at Monmouth Normal School in Monmouth, Oregon. They were both studying to be teachers. After finishing their 2 years and receiving their teaching certificates, they both got jobs in Glendale, Oregon. They became engaged and on July 31, 1937, they were married in Portland, Oregon.

Tom received a teaching job in Junction City, Oregon so after their wedding, they packed up Mary Alice's dads new 1937 Chev

LIFE AND LOVE CONTINUE

sedan with all their belongings and started out for Junction City and their new home.

Somewhere around Salem, they were in an accident and rolled the car down a hill. All their belongings, including their wedding presents were packed in that car. Only two things were damaged, a blue vegetable dish and their stand-up radio. Tom had a cut over one eye, but otherwise was not hurt. Mary Alice got out of the car and climbed back up to the highway to get help. It so happened that the first car that came by and stopped to help was someone Mary Alice knew. He was an old boyfriend. She flung her arms around his neck and started to cry. For a few seconds, she forgot that she had a new husband. Eventually, all turned out well. Old boyfriend met new husband, the car was rolled upright and pushed to the top of the hill and off they went to Junction City. I am not sure what happened to the standup radio, but I still have and use the blue vegetable dish.

When Pearl Harbor was bombed in December 1941, Tom and Mary Alice were living in a rental house in Sandy, Oregon just east of Portland. Tom was a teacher in the Milwaukie School District. Mary Alice stayed home and took care of their children; Danton Thomas born in October 1940 and Judith Ann born in October 1941. Tom was exempt from Military service because he was a teacher and he had 2 small children. He did fulfill his military obligation by working at Continental Can Company on weekends and holidays. He packed rations for the troops overseas. I can remember one Saturday when Daddy forgot his lunch. Mama piled us into the car and we drove from Southeast Portland to Northwest Portland just to take Daddy his lunch. We were able to wave at him through a basement window. The security was very heavy and we were not allowed to go in to see him. Mama had to leave his lunch at the gate and hope that he got it before someone else claimed it.

Daddy knew that he needed to finish his bachelor's degree in order to continue teaching and he wanted to get his master's degree also. His ultimate goal was to get into school administration and he would need the master's degree for that. So, in 1943, he spent his summer in Eugene, Oregon working on finishing his bachelor's degree. During the summers of 1944 and 1945, he worked on finishing up his master's degree in Elementary and Secondary education. While he was in Eugene, he stayed with good friends who lived in Springfield, OR., a small town just east of Eugene.

In the summer of 1945, Mama, Danny, and I, along with the friend from Springfield and her three children spent a month at the Oregon Coast. We drove back to Eugene to see Daddy receive his diploma.

The family returned home to Portland on V-J Day in August 1945. We had been gone from home well over a month and there was no food in the house. All the stores were closed because of the holiday. Mama told me that I got very worried that we would starve to death. The neighbor took pity on us and fed us until Mama could get to the store the next day.

Daddy became principal of Ardenwald Elementary School, in Milwaukie, Oregon, just south of Portland and Mama continued to stay home with Danny and me. When Danny started school at Woodstock School in Southeast Portland, Mama became very active in the PTA. She was attending a meeting in the Spring of 1947 where the principal was talking about their dire need for teachers in the district. Mama mentioned that she would love to return to work, but because of the law that married women could not teach, she was not able to go into the classroom and work as a paid teacher. The principal told her that if she was serious about teaching again, she needed to go to the school administration office and apply. He would hire her at Woodstock right away. She did go and apply and they hired her, but with the stipulation that she go to school and work towards getting her bachelor's degree and earning her permanent teaching certificate. So, in 1947, she started teaching first grade at Woodstock. Life changed for all of us when she went back to work. She was excited to be back to teaching but was apprehensive about the effect her teaching in the same building as Danny and I were in, would have on us. We would have to walk to school with her in the morning and stay in her classroom until it was time for the bell to ring so that we could line up and go to our own classrooms. We would have to reverse the process after school was out. We certainly didn't mind. Her room became a playroom for us.

LIFE AND LOVE CONTINUE

Danny went to Woodstock from kindergarten through the 8th grade, and I went from 1st grade through the 8th grade. Mama worked at Woodstock until her retirement in 1977. She signed up for summer school classes at Portland State College so she could finish her degree.

Woodstock school was originally established in 1891 with 12 students. In a couple of years, the attendance was up to 120 students. In 1925 the school expanded, and a second story was added. Again in 1955, the school expanded with a new cafeteria and auditorium and a new primary wing. Mama moved her classroom to the new wing. She was so excited to have water in her room and a bathroom next door. She always had a piano in her room and would play a tune to call the students to a new activity.

The same time that Mama started taking classes at Portland State, Daddy was working on his doctor's degree at Colorado Teachers College in Greeley, Colorado. So, for six years, both Daddy and Mama went to school all summer and Danny, and I lived with our grandparents. In 1952, Mama received her bachelor's degree from Portland State and Daddy received his doctor's degree from Colorado State. (Daddy's Mother and I took the train to Denver to watch Daddy receive his diploma.)

We boarded the train at Union Depot in Portland with a three-day trip to Denver ahead of us. Mama had booked a room in the sleeper car for all of us. The room had an upper and lower bunk. Mama and Danny slept on the upper bunk and Mom, and I slept on the lower bunk. Maybe Mama and Danny had good night's sleep, but I certainly did not. I was squished between the wall and my grandmother. She moved a lot and every time she turned over, she would smack me with her arm. The train ride itself seemed safe. We roamed the cars and met some interesting people. We ate in the dining car for every meal. At that time in his life, Danny was only interested in eating hamburgers. When he read the menu, they did not offer hamburgers. He was disappointed and wasn't sure what he was going to eat. Mama suggested that he try a Salisbury steak. He wasn't happy but said that he would try it. He was very surprised that it was a hamburger with gravy on it. So, he ordered Salisbury steak for both lunch and dinner for the rest of the trip.

I was glad to get off the train and see Daddy at the train station in Denver. He drove us back to Greeley. He had an apartment there that was big enough for all of us. After he received his diploma, we packed up Daddy's car and drove to Reno, Nevada to visit Aunt Polly, Uncle Dana, and Gayla. Daddy and Mom took the train back to Portland and Mama and Danny and I stayed in Reno for another week, then drove home.

In September 1952, Daddy had a massive heart attack at work. His school called Mama to let her know. They were not sure whether he was alive or not. After letting both Danny and I know, she took off for the hospital. Our grandparents came to pick us up at school. We were both too upset to finish out the day.

It took Daddy a long time to recover. It was January before he went back to work on a full-time basis. In June of 1954, Mama and Daddy decided to upgrade our living arrangements. They purchased a piece of land and had a house built. After some modifications and corrections due to poor planning on the builders' part, we moved into the house two days before Christmas, 1955.

In June 1956, Daddy was asked to be a full-time member of the faculty at Lewis and Clark College in Portland. He would be an assistant professor in the education department effective at 12:01 AM on September 1, 1956. At 12:03 AM on September 1, 1956, Daddy died of another massive heart attack. Thus, the end of the Tom and Mary Alice story.

"Doctor vs. Doctor"

My father was bordering on a narcissist. He thought very highly of himself, most of the time to the exclusion of others, including his family. When he received his PHD degree and earned the right to be called Dr. Cottingham, he wanted everyone to call him that. After his first heart attack in 1952, he would call his doctor "Mr. Berg". Finally, the doctor asked him why and he said that if Mr. Berg would call him doctor, then he would call Mr. Berg doctor. It put a strain on their relationship. I don't know if they ever resolved the problem. They probably settled on calling each other by their first names.

"Be Kind to Jimmy Day"

Mama was a special teacher. She was firm with her students, but very loving to all the children. There were parents in the school district who would beg to have their children in her classroom. After the new wing was built in 1955 and the primary classrooms were opened, the 1st grade, a 2nd grade, a split 1st and 2nd and the kindergarten class moved into the rooms. The five teachers became very close and knew each other's students as well as their own. Mama, Virginia, Bonnie, Alice, and Bernice were all at Woodstock for a long time.

Mama had a great concern for any child who had physical or emotional problems. She did not like to see children medicated for behavioral issues. She had a child Jimmy, who would come to school like a zombie. His mother only gave him the drug on school days per his doctor's instructions. After several conferences with the parents, they decided to take Jimmy off all drugs. There were a few rough days, but Mama sat down with the other students and explained that Jimmy was having a bad day and needed some extra understanding. Her students decided that what Jimmy needed was a "Be kind to Jimmy Day." It was amazing the transformation that occurred. Jimmy started to sit down quietly when asked, to read when it was his turn and not talk out of turn. And he made friends. Mama knew that he was a very smart little boy, but just did not have the ability to show it with all the medication in his body. It was amazing the caring and kindness that was expressed by the students when they understood the circumstances.

Before I was married, I would occasionally go into her classroom to read to the students or help a specific student with their work. They all seemed so eager to listen and learn and were so well behaved.

In the 30 years that Mama taught at Woodstock, she received many compliments from former students, parents, and fellow teachers. She had former students come back to see her with their children and want them in her classroom.

But probably the most important compliment that she received was from my father. He had said to a teacher at his school that there were only two first grade teachers that he would want to teach his children. One was a teacher at his school and the other was his wife. Unfortunately, he did not say it to Mama directly. It was said during a very difficult time in their marriage when they were not communicating very well. But the man that he was talking to told Mama about the comment. The comment meant a lot to her because, even though they were not getting along personally, it did show that he did value her professionally.

During her 30 years at Woodstock, she had about 10 student teachers in her classroom. She was in high demand from several of the colleges around the Portland area. She proved to be as good a teacher of prospective teachers as she was to her first graders.

Mama's career occurred before restrictions were placed on teachers that prevented them from hugging their students. Mama had long arms that enveloped a student or two and a lap that was very inviting to a child who need a little extra love and reassurance.

By the end of the school year, Mama's students were almost always ready to pass to the next grade level and Mama was always ready for her summer vacation.

Through good and honest work, life continues.

CHAPTER 7
Margaret Brunner (Nanama)

Margaret Brunner

Gentle, kind, giving, spiritual, shy, generous with time and talents and very loving. These are the traits my Nanama possessed. She was a lady in the best sense of the word. She always said that she never hated anyone. She did not know that emotion.

Nanama only had one child, Mary Alice. She wanted more but was not able to have them. From that time on, she devoted her life to Voyle, Mary Alice, Danny, and me. And how lucky we were that she did.

Margaret and Voyle were married in April 1914. Her wish at that time was to have a home for her family and settle down to being a wife, mother, and homemaker. Unfortunately, because of Voyle's work, she did not have her forever home until 1935. When they moved into the house in Southeast Portland, her mother Alice decided she would live with her daughter and son-in-law and moved in immediately. This caused some tension and chaos as Nano's sister Stella decided that she needed somewhere to live, so moved in also. More chaos!

The added stress and work caused Nanama to have a nervous breakdown. Buppa told the ladies that they would have to move. They were not happy, but Aunt Stella moved in with her son on his farm and Nano moved in with her brother IO. Margaret's health started to improve with less tension in the household. She had her home back and was able to rest and get better.

On October 23, 1940, Margaret, and Voyle's first grandchild Danton Thomas Cottingham was born. Tom and Mary Alice lived in Sandy, Oregon in a house with no heat other than a wood stove in the kitchen. The weather had turned cold, so Nanama and Buppa asked them to move into Portland with them. So, Mary Alice and Danny moved into town. Daddy stayed in Sandy during the week to go to work but was with the family on the weekends. There was no stress involved because Mama shared the workload and both grandparents reveled in their first grandchild.

Margaret went to Normal School in Lewiston, Idaho in 1912 and 1913. She took home economics with an emphasis on cooking. She did become a very accomplished cook. Even though money was very tight, she was able to put together a beautiful meal that was always beautifully presented. She had a tablecloth with matching napkins, silverware in the perfect spots and some sort of centerpiece on the table. salt, pepper, sugar and cream and a butter dish with butter knife were in their proper place. The meal was often the simplest of meals, but she always made you feel like a special honored guest.

During the lean Depression years, Voyle was often paid in produce. They were living and working in farm country in Western Oregon. One payday, Voyle was paid with a 50-pound bag of onions.

LIFE AND LOVE CONTINUE

Nanama made the best of the situation and made a variety of dishes with onions and apparently, they were perfection.

Nanama had the best lap to crawl onto—she could bandage a scraped knee and kiss away the hurt better than anyone. She would always give an extra hug.

On April 12, 1957, Nanama left her home for the last time. When Buppa died, we knew that she would not be able to care for herself and moved her into our house. She deeply mourned Buppa for 6 years until her death in August 1963.

"Fudge and Divinity"

In the 1940's and 1950's, my grandparents did not have a lot of discretionary money. They pretty much lived from payday to payday. The only income they had was Buppa's railroad pay. At Christmas, things were even more financially tight for them. Christmas presents were not an option, so Nanama made fudge and divinity to give as gifts. She would spend hours in the kitchen making her candy. Her fudge was the kind that had to be kneaded, which made it so smooth and incredible tasting. When she made the divinity, she whipped the egg whites by hand as she drizzled in the hot syrup. She did have an electric mixer but did not use it for her divinity. Both Nanama and Buppa would package and wrap the boxes and would give them to the men in the family. The men would receive their presents, kiss Nanama on the cheek and immediately head for their cars to put the box in their car. Danny and I could never figure out why they did not open their presents right away. We were older when we realized that their presents were the candy and if it was opened, they would have to share it with everyone. As with all her cooking, Nanama's candy was the best.

"Canning and Jelly Making"

In 1937, Voyle and Margaret bought their forever home in Southeast Portland. The house was a mansion to them compared to some of the places they had lived. They had lived in one room in someone else's home, in a shack in the woods and even a train caboose. To have a home of their own was a dream come true.

The house had two bedrooms on the main floor with a second floor and a basement. The basement had a blocked off area with shelves from floor to ceiling available for canned goods. Nanama, being the homemaker that she was, vowed to keep them full of fruits and vegetables, jams and jellies.

Their property had a peach tree, an apple tree, a pear tree, and a pie cherry tree. All the trees were good producers and provided Nanama with lots of fruit to can in the Summer. She had a 7-quart pressure cooker, and she kept it busy all summer.

As the fruit became ripe, Buppa would pick it and bring it into the house where Nanama would process it. She would, almost every year, can 60 to 70 quarts of peaches. With only a 7-quart pressure cooker it took her quite a few days to complete the canning of a specific fruit. Not only would she can the fruit right off the tree, but she made applesauce and her own fruit cocktail. She also would can vegetables that Buppa grew. Green beans, peas, corn, tomatoes, and cucumber pickles were some of the vegetables that went on the shelves in the basement. All this activity occurred during the heat of the summer. Nanama would stand at the kitchen sink with a towel around her head so the sweat would not drip into the jars.

During all this activity, the berries would get ripe. Buppa's brother Earl had a farm just south of Portland. He grew strawberries, raspberries loganberries, and gooseberries. My favorites were the blackcaps. Nanama would make jam or jelly out of all types of berries, sometimes combining them to make unusual flavors.

When it was jelly making time, Nanama would bake bread in the morning and we would have warm bread and the skimming's off the blackcap jelly for breakfast. I can taste it now.

I would sit on a tall stool beside her most of the time she was working. She never complained that I was in the way, although sometimes I probably was, and she would teach me in the simplest ways as she was processing all of the bounty. As I grew older, I was able to help her more. I did not realize how much knowledge about canning I had absorbed until I started canning for my family. How fortunate I was to have the option to freeze food as well. Thanks, Nanama for the love and care you put into every jar of food you put on those shelves.

With love and sometimes hard work, life continues.

CHAPTER 8

What we know of Tom and his Family

Tom Cottingham

Tom was born on April 20, 1913, in Hamilton, Texas to Jesse and Estella Cottingham. He had 1 older sister. They moved to Richland, Washington where his brother Richard was born. Sometime before Tom was in the first grade, they emigrated to Alberta, Canada. Tom attended first grade in Lethbridge, Alberta.

LIFE AND LOVE CONTINUE

From Lethbridge, it is assumed that only Estella and her children returned to the United States, coming to Portland, Oregon. Jesse joined the Canadian Military and served in World War I.

Tom attended Creston elementary and Franklin High schools in Portland. At some point during that time, Helen was disowned by her mother. Tom saw her a few times, but after he was married and his children were born, communication ceased.

Tom went to college at Monmouth Normal School in Monmouth, Oregon and received his teaching certificate. He received his bachelor's and master's degrees at the University of Oregon.

Tom's brother Ted (he legally changed his name from Richard to Ted) joined the Navy and served in Alaska during World War II.

Tom met Mary Alice Brunner in college at Monmouth. They both received teaching positions in Glendale, Oregon.

Tom was a very good-looking man and attracted a lot of attention from women. They flocked around him when he was young and continued to do so until he died.

He was an educator, going to school until he received his PHD in 1952. His goal was to become an administrator and to teach at the college level. He expressed many times that he thought teaching was a much more important profession than some others because he would be forming the minds of students who would lead our country into the future. When he got into the college level of teaching, he was training the people who would then be teaching those young students.

During our young years, Mama and Daddy would argue, thinking that we could not hear them, but we did. Even their attitude towards each other after an argument would show us that something was wrong. His mother had told him to marry, if not for love, then for appearance's sake. She thought that being married would advance his career. Sometimes he would yell at Mama that she had been the most convenient person to marry.

Manual labor was foreign to Daddy, especially jobs around the house. When we lived in the first house in Portland and Danny and I were very little, there was no central heating. They relied on the kitchen wood stove to heat the entire house. In the winter, they had to keep the fire going all night long. Mama had moved our beds into the kitchen alcove so that we were nearer the heat. There were times when Daddy would come home from work, lay down on the sofa and go to sleep. Mama needed wood for the stove so that she could fix dinner, but he told her to get it herself. He was tired because he had worked all day and she hadn't. She would have to bundle Danny and me up, take us outside with her, chop wood and bring it into the house. She could not leave us in the house near the fire and Daddy would not watch us.

When we moved to the first house they owned, she was so excited about the electric stove in the kitchen and the oil furnace. No more chopping wood for her.

Money was very tight right after the war, but when cars became available for the public to buy, Daddy bought a new car, and he bought one about every two years from then on, plus he had a new suit every year. His appearance was very important to him. At the same time, Mama had to ask for 50 cents to buy and new pair of underpants. And forget new clothes for Danny and me. Since Mama was a very good seamstress, she took old clothes and made them into new outfits for us. It wasn't until after she started working that she felt comfortable spending any money on herself, and then it was not very much. Her paycheck was needed for food and utilities.

The time before Daddy's first heart attack was very difficult for them. He had asked for a divorce, but Mama would not give him one. He had a girlfriend in Colorado and apparently wanted to be with her. When he came home from the hospital, he was confined to a hospital bed set up in the dining room. While Mama was working during the day, Daddy had a visiting nurse, but the minute Mama came home, the nurse left and Mama took care of him, along with taking care of Danny and me. That was when I learned to help in the kitchen. I would get home from school before she would and get dinner started.

Daddy was not supposed to drive, but one-day Mama came home and found Daddy and his car gone. When he came home, she was livid and wanted to know where he had been. He was out getting something to eat. He said that there was nothing in the house he wanted to eat. She had worked very hard to have food available for him while she was gone. Mama told him that he could have his divorce, she was through catering to him, but he decided that he did not want a divorce. He apologized for scaring her and he wanted to repair their marriage. After some intensive therapy and time spent together, they did repair their fractured marriage.

Daddy was a very good teacher and administrator and every few years, he would take a couple of months off from his administrative job and go back into the classroom and teach, sometimes elementary classes and sometimes high school classes.

He was a good teacher but not a very good father. He did not participate or attend our school functions, nor did he help Danny when he was in Cub Scouts. In other words, he pretty much ignored us.

Daddy was very quiet and did not speak of his family or his life before he married Mama. He did not have a close loving relationship with his mother. He did visit her occasionally and she was at our home once in a while, but they were not easy visits. Daddy died of a massive heart attack on September 1, 1956.

Not all of my memories of my father are good ones and I felt that I had to include the bad memories also.

Even thru adversity, Life continues.

CHAPTER 9
Estella Mitchell Cottingham (Mom)

I had another grandmother, Estella Cottingham. We called her "Mom". She was my father's mother. We did not see her often and when we did, it was usually a strained visit.

She was born in Streator, Illinois in 1893. Nothing is known about her young life, how she met her husband, Jesse Cottingham or how and why they came west. I do know that her father's name was Ira and her mother's name was Clara.

LIFE AND LOVE CONTINUE

We do know that she and Jesse had three children, Helen, Thomas, and Richard. Thomas was born in Hamilton, Texas and Richard was born in Richland, Washington. We know nothing about Helen. She was apparently "disowned" by her mother, why we do not know.

Thomas, my dad, went to the first grade in Lethbridge, Alberta, Canada. We think that from there, Estella and the three children went to Portland. Jesse remained in Canada and joined the Canadian Military serving in Europe in WWI. We do know that he remained in Canada and is buried in Calgary, Alberta

Both Thomas and Richard went to Creston Elementary School and Franklin High School in Portland.

Estella (Mom) lived in a small apartment on N.E. Couch Street in Portland and worked as a seamstress in a laundry in downtown Portland.

Occasionally, Daddy would take us to see her. We would walk in; Daddy would hug his mother and sit down on the sofa. She would sit in her overstuffed chair in the living room. Soon Daddy would lay down on the sofa and go to sleep and Mom would sit and crochet. She made beautiful, intricate lace tablecloths. Danny and I would sit at the kitchen table with nothing to do and had to ask to use her bathroom. We were never offered even a glass of water. She did consent to give us each a piece of paper and a pencil. We usually played "tic-tac-toe" or "hangman". After about an hour, Daddy would wake up, visit with his mother for a few minutes and then we would leave. Danny and I did not enjoy those visits.

I remember a few times she came to our house for a meal. One Christmas she stayed overnight. She wore a lavender housecoat that Mama had made for her, and she wore it all day. Mom did not like cats, but our kitten loved her. Tammy cat would jump up on her lap whenever she sat down. She finally became very attached to the cat and wouldn't let us take her off her lap.

Mom happened to be staying overnight at our house when Daddy died. She blamed Mama for his death. She felt that Mama expected too much from him and he worked himself to death to please her. Mama made sure that Mom was included in the arrangements for the funeral so she would not feel left out and so she would know that Mama did care about Daddy.

The day of Daddy's funeral was the last time we saw her. Mama tried to reach out to her several times, but she never reciprocated. She died on July 29, 1958. I read about her death in the newspaper. My uncle Ted did not feel that it was necessary to inform us. Mama had remarried and he thought that we were no longer a part of her family. I was sorry she died, but since she had made no effort to contact us or answer Mama's calls, I did not miss her.

But Life Does Continue.

CHAPTER 10

4306 S. E. Ramona

Danny and Judy—1944

Our house at 4306 S. E. Ramona in Portland, Oregon had a large porch across the front with the door in the middle. As you walked in the door, there was a hallway and stairs to the second floor. The staircase was very wide and there were 15 steps. On the right was my parents' bedroom and on the left was the living room. From their bedroom, you could walk into the bathroom and through that to the kitchen. The dining room was on the far side of the living room.

The door from the front hallway to the living room was always open, except for Christmas Eve and Christmas morning. On Christmas Eve, Danny and I had to go to bed by 7:00 pm so we would be asleep when Santa Claus came. That was the time when my parents brought in the tree and decorated it and put out the presents. Presents from Santa were never wrapped.

On Christmas morning, we would come downstairs only to find the door still closed. We could go through the bedroom to the bathroom, but no further. We had to wait until our grandparents and great-grandma and great uncle got there. Nanama and Buppa would go pick them up and they were usually there by 7:30, but it was a very long wait for two anxious kids.

As soon as they arrived and had their coffee or tea and were settled, the door was opened, and we would see the tree for the first time. I remember tricycles, dolls, train sets and especially the J.C. Higgins bikes—one blue and one red. Oh, how excited we were.

There were wonderful smells coming from the kitchen. Mama would make us a light breakfast because if Christmas fell on any day but Monday and Tuesday, we had to eat by 2:00 pm. Buppa had to go to work at 4:00. Mondays and Tuesdays were his days off. If Christmas fell on one of those days, we had dinner at Nanama and Buppa's house. That would be a special time. All the cousins would come later in the day.

As Danny and I got older and no longer believed in Santa, we could help decorate the tree on Christmas Eve. The door was still closed on Christmas morning though. I remember one Christmas when I was 12. I was sick and was sleeping on the sofa so I would be closer to Mama. On Christmas morning, Daddy and the neighbor came in carrying a beautiful white cedar chest. It was the most beautiful thing I had ever seen. The next year I got the matching dresser and nightstand. I thought I was the most grownup girl ever. I still use that dresser.

Daddy never liked the idea of having two Christmas trees in one year, so the tree would come down on the morning of New Year's Eve. Danny and I usually helped to dismantle the tree. All the ornaments were either glass or cardboard and had to be carefully wrapped and stored in the boxes. Then the tinsel had to be taken off and put back on the cardboard holder that it came in. What a job.

LIFE AND LOVE CONTINUE

The memories of those Christmases are so special to me and during the holiday time, are so vivid. I treasure the times we had as a family.

Mama and Daddy had been talking for some time about remodeling the kitchen. To save money, Daddy decided to do the work himself. So, one evening about 8:30 PM, I woke up to the sound of pounding. I came downstairs and saw Daddy on a chair with a crowbar in his hand, ripping apart the ceiling in the kitchen. You have got to understand that my father had no skill in carpentry at all. Mama was trying to tell him that the ceiling was not the best place to start the project, that maybe they had best take things out of the cupboards and off the walls first. He finally agreed that was the best way to start.

One day when the major construction was complete and Mama was doing the painting, she fainted. I walked into the kitchen to find Daddy had thrown a soaking wet washcloth on her face. I asked him if he had killed her when she came up sputtering and hollering that she could not breathe with that damned wet cloth on her face. That was probably the first time I had ever heard my mother swear.

The toaster we had was an old fashioned one where each side went down so that the bread could be put in and toasted. You had to watch it very carefully for it not to burn. I had somewhat of a history with that toaster. During the last week of the month before payday, our dinners often consisted of oatmeal and toast. Before the kitchen was remodeled, we had to put the toaster on the table and run the cord to the electrical outlet. I got up from the table once and ran into the cord, knocking the toaster off the table. Daddy was so mad that he swatted me and sent me to my room. He came into my room a little later to explain to me why he spanked me. We had no money to buy a new toaster and that one was necessary to prepare our meals. He was able to fix it though and it gave us a few more years of use. That was the first and only time that my father spanked me.

About a month after the kitchen remodel was completed, I came home from school and wanted some cinnamon toast for a snack. I put the bread in the toaster, then went into the living room to call my grandma. When I hung up the phone, I smelled something funny, went into the kitchen and saw the toast burning and the underneath of the cupboards scorched. I had forgotten to pull the toaster out from under the cupboard. I felt miserable and had to tell my parents what I had done to their brand new kitchen. Fortunately, they were relieved that I was okay and the house did not burn down. The next day, we had a new toaster and Mama refinished the cupboards and no one could see that I almost burned the house down. To this day, I always pull the toaster out from under the cupboards and always make sure the smoke alarms work.

"Margarine and Friends"

It was rare when we could cross the street in front of our house. We lived on a corner lot and even in the 1940's, cars went fast, and we had to be super careful. Across the street and down the next block was the corner grocery store. A new product was in the stores and Mama wanted to try it. It was called Oleo Margarine, so she would take us across the street, and we would walk to the store to buy the margarine. Mama would call Mrs. Burgess, the owner of the store and let her know we were coming. The margarine was white when we got it and it was encased in a sealed plastic bag. There was a dye packet in the margarine and Mrs. Burgess would pop the packet and Danny and I would knead the margarine while we were walking home. Mama was always at the corner to walk us back across the street. The margarine was yellow by the time we were home.

When we were a little older and could cross the street by ourselves and it was hot outside, Mama would give us each a penny and we would walk to the store for a penny popsicle. To us, nothing tasted as good on a hot day as that popsicle.

My friend Lynny lived with her grandma in a huge house on the way to the corner store. When I was in the second grade, I could go play at her house. The house was so large that it had four floors—a basement, a main floor, a second floor and an attic. The attic was where we played most of the time. There were clothes to wear for dress up and corners to sit and play with our dolls or color. Lynny and I would spend hours up there. We were good friends for a long time. After graduation from high school, I was maid of honor in her wedding. At some point in our growing up years, I started calling her Lynn, but in my mind, she will always be Lynny.

I had another good friend, Marilyn. We became good friends in the fourth grade, although I had known her since first grade. When I was in the fourth grade, I walked to school instead of riding with Mama and Marilyn's house was on the way to school. We would usually meet up while we were walking. Marilyn and I would color together and play dress up. We drifted apart when we got into high school. I was taking classes to prepare for college, and she was going to get married 5 days after graduation. Our interests were a lot different by that time. Even though we were not the best of friends anymore, she was the only person I wanted to see when Daddy died. Her mother brought her to our house and she and I spent most of the day together. I will always be grateful for her support.

"Telephones and Party Lines"

Shortly after we moved into our house, my parents had a telephone installed. There were two other families who were on our line. At first, we had to go get them to come to our house to take their call, but after a while they got their own equipment. The phone company had different rings for the people on the line. Our ring was three long rings. We knew it was a call for us when we would hear that ring.

If we wanted to make a call and someone else was on the line, we had to wait until they were finished with their call. It was always so tempting to listen in on their conversations, but we didn't. Private lines were very hard to come by, but as soon as one was available, Daddy got one. He did not like waiting to make his phone call. Our first phone number was Tabor 4311. We had that number until the phone company added zones and went to an all-numerical system.

"Pinochle and Bedtimes"

Our house had a large heat register on the main floor between the living room and the dining room. Directly above the register was a vent that went into my bedroom. The heat would rise and keep my room warm. Danny and I could lay on the floor and watch what was going on at the table in the dining room.

My parents had some special friends that liked to play pinochle with them. On pinochle nights we would be fed and rushed off to bed early so that Mama could get the company dinner fixed and the table set. After dinner they would play pinochle. Mama usually made a special dinner and Danny and I did not get any until the next day. We ate the leftovers. During the pinochle games, we would lay on the floor and watch them play. We did not understand the rules of the game, but we had a lot of fun watching. We were supposed to be in bed, but I am sure our parents knew we were there.

"Bedtime"

From as far back as I can remember, our bedtime was 7:30 pm both summer and winter. We were in the 5th grade before we could stay up later. Danny and I thought it was terribly unfair to have to go to bed so early, especially in the Summer when all the other kids were outside playing, and we could hear them. But no matter where we were or what we were doing, we were bathed and ready for bed at 7:30.

During the Summer, there were too many fun things going on outside for us to be cooped up in our bedrooms. The high school kids would be out playing soft ball in the intersection. And some of the girls would be sitting on their front porches playing with paper dolls. Most of these kids were out until 8:00 or 9:00, but here were the poor "Cottingham" kids, in bed by 7:30. As with the heat register peeking, we would be hanging our heads out the window in Danny's bedroom watching the evening activities in the neighborhood. It was a joyous day when we could be outside with them.

Car vs. Table

In the Spring of 1952, Daddy bought a new car. It wasn't a surprise to us because he bought a new car every two years.

Mama blew up at this purchase though. She had been trying to get him to agree on a new dining room table for quite a while and he said they didn't need one. The table they had was in the house when they bought it and was a homemade one that wobbled. There were four mismatched chairs. Daddy did not feel we needed a new table. Mama could cover up the table with a tablecloth and put something under the table leg to stop the wobbling. Mama informed him that if he bought a new car, she was going to buy a new table and it was not going to be a cheap one. She went shopping and bought a beautiful solid cherry wood trestle table with 6 chairs and a buffet to match.

Daddy kept the car and Mama kept the table. Daddy did admit that the table was very nice, and a truce was called.

I have had the table, chairs, and buffet for 50 years. A lot of people have had a lot of meals at that table. It has lasted thru my brother, me, my three children and my seven grandchildren and will last a lot longer. The car did not last. He bought a new one 2 years later.

"Broken Glass"

Danny and I grew up being the best of friends. We were only four days less than a year apart and were raised like twins. We looked out for each other, and we never fought like a lot of brothers and sisters. But we did tease each other occasionally.

When we were 9 years old, we could walk home from school by ourselves and not have to wait for Mama. Most of the time we walked together but sometimes we wanted to be alone. One of the rules we had to keep, was to lock the doors and not let anyone in the house until either Mama or Daddy got home. Well, Danny walked by himself one day and got home before I did. He locked the door and would not let me in. He stood at the window in the back door and laughed at me. He knew that the first thing I did when I got home was go to the bathroom. He would not let me in, and I was getting more and more desperate. I started pounding on the glass and was pounding harder and harder the worse I had to go. I pounded so hard, I put my fist through the window.

Danny was standing in the kitchen with his face right up to the window when the glass shattered. I had small cuts on my hands, but miraculously, he was not hurt. Boy were we scared! We were both crying and hugging each other. The worst thing was that I wet my pants. After cleaning up my cuts and sweeping up the glass, we had to sit and wait for our parents to come home. We paid for the glass out of our allowance and Buppa came the next day and put the new glass in.

Danny and I swore that we would never fight again, and we didn't. If we had any kind of disagreement, we would talk it out. It was much safer.

"The Dreaded Piano Lessons"

When Danny and I were in the second and third grades, one of my aunts loaned my Mama a big upright player piano. Mama thought it was time for us to have an appreciation for music. So, we started piano lessons on Thursdays after school. We walked across the street from the school where the lady taught the classes.

Danny did very well and had the ability to move his hands quickly. I didn't! I struggled. When we first started lessons, I was sure that in a couple of lessons I would be able to play anything I wanted to. What a letdown. I started doing scales. For months it seemed like all I did were scales and learning the keys. And, if I made a mistake, the teacher would flick my arm with her thumb and forefinger. And oh, did I hate to practice.

After 8 years of suffering this torture, I convinced Mama that I was not going to get any better and it was a waste of money to pay for lessons that were not helping. So, I didn't take lessons anymore and Mama gave the piano back to Aunt Stella. I played my grandparents piano sometimes when I was at their house, but was not very enthusiastic about it.

When I got into high school, I loved the popular songs and would go to the music store and buy the sheet music for the songs I wanted. After Buppa died, their piano came to our house, so I was

LIFE AND LOVE CONTINUE

able to play anytime I wanted to. I taught myself to chord and if the music had the guitar chords on it, I could usually figure out the song.

I am 80 years old now and fervently wish that I had practiced and paid more attention to those lessons.

Life Certainly does Continue.

CHAPTER 11

About 3 years after Mama started teaching again, she had to have kidney surgery. She wasn't going to be able to take care of the household chores for several weeks and Daddy was not willing to cook and clean, so Aunt Dede paid for her cleaning lady to come once a week to clean and do the washing and ironing. Her name was Josephine (Jo). She was such a help and Daddy said the house had never looked so good. He thought Jo did a better job of ironing his shirts than mama did. Mama hated to iron! He decided that we needed Jo to come on a permanent basis. So, every Friday until 1965, Jo would come to clean. She quickly became a member of the family.

Events seemed to happen on Fridays in our family and Jo was always there. Daddy had his first heart attack on a Friday and Jo was there. She was there when we moved into our new home in 1955. She was there on the Friday that Daddy died, and she was the one who came to school to let me now that Buppa died.

It was a Friday when I moved into the dorm at college. She helped me move in and put my stuff away. She even made my bed for me.

When Nanama came to live with us in 1957, Jo became her companion. She would fix her meals on Fridays and would take care of her needs.

It was a sad day when Jo no longer came to our house, but she was physically unable to do the work anymore. We all missed her but were so grateful she had been a part of our family for as long as she was.

Life goes on as it should.

CHAPTER 12

Portland's Union Station (The Depot)

Portland's Union Station was a magical place to me. Buppa worked there as a telegrapher. He started working there in 1936 and was there until his retirement in 1955. He worked the 4:00pm to 12:00 midnight shift for all the years he was there. Mondays and Tuesdays were his days off. It was special for him to be able to stay in one place after being bumped around so much during the depression.

Occasionally, he would take me to work with him on Friday evening. All the employees knew Buppa and I pretty much had free reign of the place, but could not disturb any employees who were working and absolutely could not go through the doors to the train platform. I also had to stay in the office when a train was coming in or going out. There were a lot of people milling around at those times.

When it was supper time, Buppa would open up the supper that Nanama had made for us (usually leftovers from our 2:00 pm dinner) and then he would take me down to the diner for a special treat. The waitress would make me a huge hot fudge sundae with all the trimmings on it. Buppa and I would share the sundae. As I write this, can see that sundae.

Buppa was an artist and could see pictures in the marble walls and floor. He taught me how to look for pictures in clouds, in the marble walls, in trees. When I was walking around the depot by myself, I would find pictures everywhere.

During July and August, the trains would come in from Hermiston, Oregon loaded with the big Hermiston watermelons. A lot of them were broken in transit and could not be sold, so they would give them away to the depot employees. Buppa would fill the trunk of his car with those watermelons and we would feast on them for days. Buppa would cut the melon in four pieces. We would only eat the heart of the melon and throw the rest away.

Buppa retired in 1955 and his retirement party was held in a conference room at the Depot. There were about 50 people there and several of his fellow workers put on a skit, "This is your Life, Voyle Brunner." It was very funny. The best part of the party was the serving of the cake. The cake was shaped like the depot and there were little people walking into the building. Buppa was at the front door directing people. It was a fun party.

That party was the last time I was in the depot with him.

And Life Goes On.

CHAPTER 13

Living with Grandparents

Multnomah falls picnic

From the Summer of 1948 until the Summer of 1952, Danny and I lived with our Grandparents during the summer. We were there from June to the middle of August. Daddy was going to school in Greeley, Colorado working towards his Doctor of Education degree and Mama was going to Portland State working to complete her permanent teaching certificate and her bachelor's degree in Elementary Education. Because there was no one at our house to take care of us, we moved in with Nanama and Buppa. It was no hardship for us. We loved being there. It was like our second home.

There were some mysteries about their house. It had a second floor where Danny slept. The only problem was that there was no floor—only the rafters and the downstairs ceiling. Buppa had put some plywood down so Danny could have a place to sleep and play, but we had to be very careful about walking around up there.

There were so many things stored up there. There were books, boxes of papers, lots of pictures propped up against the walls, lots of trunks full of clothes and papers. There were bits and pieces of rolled up carpet. There was a large box of Christmas decorations. When Danny and I were very little, we thought that Santa came back and took the decorations back to the North Pole. There was one great box of clothes that I loved to play dress up in. There was a trunk with a lot of Buppa's artwork in it. He took correspondent classes and the pictures in the trunk were the returned pictures with the critique on them and the grade. They were so much fun to look at.

Another fun place to play was the basement. The washer and dryer were down there along with Buppa's work bench and tools. There was also a walled off portion of the basement full of shelves for canned goods. There was a big sawdust furnace and a separate sawdust room. Buppa usually had sawdust delivered once a year in the summer. He would remove the window from the room and it was blown in from a large hose inserted into the open space. It took about a half hour for that room to fill up. First, Danny and I would sit outside and watch the men get the truck and hose ready to fill the room, then we would rush into the basement and watch the room fill with sawdust. We couldn't go into the room. We would have been buried in sawdust very quickly.

There always seemed to be so much to do at Nanama and Buppa's house. There was a large side yard to play in. Buppa had two good sized gardens—one in the side yard and one in the parking area at the other side of the house. It was between the sidewalk and the street. Both gardens needed a lot of care, so being the innocent children that we were, we weeded. We made a contest of it to see who could pull the most weeds. Nanama usually had a treat for the one who got the most. She would usually declare a tie so that each of us got some of the treat.

In the middle of the summer when it was very hot, Buppa would put up the tepee that he made, and we would sleep out there. Danny would wear his cowboy outfit and Nanama would braid my hair like an Indian girl. Those are such good memories.

Their yard had a peach tree, an apple tree, a pear tree and a pie cherry tree and they were all good producers.

Every year, Nanama would process many quarts of fruit. One of our great joys every summer was standing under the peach tree limbs, eating the peaches right off the tree. We would be covered in peach juice and must run for the house so the bees would not get us. We thought we were being so sneaky, but Nanama always knew because of the condition of our clothes. They were covered in peach juice and dirt. No peach that I eat now can compare to those.

When we were very young, Nanama and Buppa had an ice box in their kitchen instead of a refrigerator. That meant the ice man came to deliver a block of ice. At first, the ice man drove a wagon pulled by a horse. That was always a treat for us to be able to give the horse a carrot. After a while, he would drive a gas-powered truck. We were sad that we could not see the horse anymore. All the kids in the neighborhood would gather in front of our house and wait for the sliver of ice we would get just before the wagon left. About 2 years later, they got an electric refrigerator and there was no more iceman.

Their house was built on a corner lot with a five-foot bank at the front and side of the house. One of our great pleasures was rolling down that bank. We would roll down, then climb the front steps and roll down again. I am surprised that Nanama let us continue to do that. She had a lot of grass stains to get out of our clothes.

Sometimes, Buppa would want to go on a picnic. One of our favorite places to go was Multnomah Falls. Buppa had Mondays and Tuesdays off work so our mini trips would be on one of those days. Nanama would pack a picnic lunch for us, and we would drive up the Columbia River Highway in Buppa's 1937 Chev. The highway was narrow and full of curves and was a challenge to drive, but the scenery was beautiful. There were eight water falls along the way, but all of them were not visible from the road. We would stop at as many as we could see. We always made a stop at Crown Point and the Vista House. It is a hexagon building very high up on a cliff. The highway runs right by it. The view of the Columbia River both East and West is incredible. Buppa called it the "Million Dollar Pee Pot". That is how much it cost to build it. It had one of the few bathrooms along the highway from Gresham to the Multnomah Falls Lodge.

The next big excitement for us was to round the corner and see Multnomah Falls Lodge, then the Falls itself. The Lodge is a stone building that houses a hotel, a restaurant, a gift shop, and public bathrooms.

The falls are divided in two by a shelf of land and a small lake. There is a bridge across the break in the upper and the lower falls. The upper falls is very high, and the lower falls is much shorter. We would climb to the bridge, then head back to the picnic table that Nanama had chosen for us. It was usually on the stream that ran into the Columbia River.

Nanama believed in setting the table whether we were at home or on a picnic. We had a tablecloth, napkins, plates and silverware, cups or glasses and at that time, they did not have paper plates or plastic silverware, so she used the real thing. She would have the salt, pepper, sugar and cream available. There was always a thermos of coffee for Buppa and milk for Danny and me. Our meal was usually a meat: chicken or ham, potato salad, deviled eggs, an apple or pear, bread, or a roll, then desert, either pie, cake, or cookies. We did have a complete meal, even though we were on a picnic.

Danny would finish eating and he would go off to fish in the stream. He did more fishing than catching but had a lot of fun anyway. I would try and find flat rocks that I could skip across the water. I didn't have much luck either. I had not perfected the talent—Never did! Soon it was time to pack up and leave. Danny and I were usually asleep by the time we got home.

LIFE AND LOVE CONTINUE

We really did not miss our parents too much during the Summer. Mama would come for supper several times a week and get caught up on our activities. We talked to Daddy on July 31st. That was their wedding anniversary and he always called on that day. They both knew that we would have a good summer and were safe.

My grandparents did not believe in medical doctors. They leaned towards Christian Science beliefs and studied Naturopathic and Chiropractic medicine. When I was nine years old, I got very sick. My parents both had to work and could not stay home with me, and they did not have health insurance for Danny and me. My grandparents offered to take care of me as long as they could pursue their medical beliefs. My parents really did not have much of a choice.

So, I moved into Nanama and Buppa's house in January 1950 and was there until June 1950. I started a bizarre course of treatment. They took me to a Naturopath/Chiropractor every day for treatment. Dr. Burke's office was in downtown Portland, so Buppa would drive downtown every morning, park the car in a secure lot and we would walk to the doctor's office. He would give me an adjustment, then the weird treatment would start. First, he would stick his finger down my throat so I would throw up. This got all the impurities out of my system. Then he would run water into my nose to clean it out. He would clean my ears out also. By the time the treatment was over, I should have been clean enough to do surgery. After the treatment, we would go into his office, and he would have several more vitamins and minerals for me to take. They had to pay the bill each day. The doctor would not bill by the month. Knowing now how tight money was for them, I am surprised that they spent so much on my treatments. I am sure my mother did not know either. She never would have let them spend that much.

Mama finally decided that I was getting better, but needed a medical doctor's care, so I moved back home when school was out, and she was around to take care of me. I went to the medical doctor, and he put me on some antibiotics and within a very short time I was much better.

I had missed half a year of school, so I had to go to summer school to make up the time I lost. It was not fun, but it was either that or be held back and redo the fourth grade the next school year. We opted for Summer School. I had to study hard to pass the class.

Life Definitely Continues.

CHAPTER 14

Vacations with Mama and Daddy

Cannon Beach

Two weeks before school started in the Fall, Daddy would come home from Colorado and Mama would be finished with her classes, so we would be off to Cannon Beach on the Oregon Coast. That was our favorite place - our Happy Place. We stayed at the "Singing Sands" cabin every year. Daddy would reserve it for the next year before we left. It was a 2-bedroom cabin with kitchen eating area, and a large living room with a huge fireplace. The door let out onto the beach and the view of the ocean was unobstructed.

Mama usually took her sewing machine, along with all the accessories needed and lots of fabric and she would make school clothes for both of us. Daddy took a whole box full of books to read. He read so many textbooks during the summer, that he wanted to read "fun" books for a change. He would sit in front of the fire and read most of the day. Danny and I would play in the sand all day. We would build sandcastles, dig to China, have races, search for agates and whole sand dollars and pretty rocks.

Right after the war ended, the Navy and the Coast Guard were still patrolling the shoreline. We would see four or five grey ships on the horizon at a time. Mama said that they had to be there to keep us safe. One year when we got to the beach, they were no longer there. We were told that they were no longer needed. We were going to remain safe now.

Daddy loved Cannon Beach. One October Friday evening at about 8:00 PM, he got Danny and I up from bed and piled us all in the car, drove to his mother's apartment and picked her up and we went for a drive. Danny and I were asleep again very quickly but woke up when we got to Cannon Beach. We started to get out of the car, but Daddy told us to stay there. He walked down to the water's edge, went to the bathroom in the ocean and then came back to the car. He started up and drove back home to Portland. When his mother asked him why we drove all the way to the beach, he said "I have always wanted to pee in the Ocean. When we are here in the Summer, there are always too many people around."

Our last trip to Cannon Beach as a family was in August 1952. In September, Daddy had a massive heart attack. He was in the hospital for a month, home in a hospital bed for another month and then on restricted activity until after Christmas. Restricted activity meant no driving. It was January before he was able to return to work and then with light duty only. Life changed for us when he had that heart attack. No more trips to Cannon Beach.

"Grapeview on Puget Sound"

In 1952, when Daddy was recovering from his heart attack, his doctor told him that he needed to exercise on a consistent basis. He decided to learn to play golf and went out and bought a complete set of clubs and all the accessories. He signed up for lessons and off he went. Mama did not want to be a golf widow, so she took up golf too. Daddy bought her a complete set of clubs and accessories and signed her up for lessons at the same time as his. That started their obsession with golf.

In August 1954, instead of Cannon Beach for our vacation, we went to Grapeview, WA, a small town between Tacoma and Olympia right on the Puget Sound waters. Some good friends of Mama and Daddy had a cabin there and they were golfers also. They spend a few hours every day playing golf either at the Shelton, WA course or the Bremerton, WA course. Danny and I would usually stay behind. He would fish and I would either do jig saw puzzles, play with my dolls,

LIFE AND LOVE CONTINUE

or read. It would get boring for us because there were no other kids around and we were in the middle of the woods. We were not even within walking distance of the city.

In August of 1954, we took an additional 2-week vacation and drove down the Oregon Coast almost to the California border then went East to the Oregon Caves. Daddy drove us up to the entrance, but because of the altitude, he was not able to go on the tour with us. He drove us up there, went to a lower altitude and in about an hour, came back to get us. I remember very little of the tour, just that it was very cold. It was the middle of the Summer, so we were dressed appropriately. But we were not dressed correctly for climbing around in an underground cave. It was good to get to the top again.

From the caves, we drove to Crater Lake. Even Danny and I were impressed. We did not stay overnight at the lake but drove around it. Daddy took a lot of pictures with his new camera. A lot of years later, Mama painted one of his pictures. It was one of the first oil paintings that she did. From Crater Lake, we drove up to Bend and then into Eugene and home to Portland. We had a fun, relaxing trip and I do remember being happy.

Mama and Daddy took the Summer of 1955 off from school and teaching and played golf all summer. They played on just about every small course from Astoria to Brookings and back up Highway 99. They managed to heal their fractured marriage and were able to spend some quality time together.

We were home for a week and then headed for Grapeview. One of their favorite courses to play was Shelton, WA. It was a small 9-hole course, and they would usually play 2 rounds. One of the tees is high up on a hill and the green is just below the hill. You cannot see the green from the tee. Daddy teed off and when he got to the green, could not find his ball. Finally, Mama found it in the cup. He had made a whole-in-one. What was weird was that on the next round, he did the same thing.

Danny loved to fish and would take the little rowboat out onto the sound and fish. He had certain limits as to how far out he could go. He was very good about staying within his limits. I did not like the water, so I would not go with him. I remember a time when he was out in the boat and Daddy said that he supposed he needed to be a father to his son. He went to the water's edge, called at Danny to row to shore. Daddy climbed in and Danny rowed back out to fish some more. About 30 minutes later, Danny rowed back in, Daddy got out of the boat and came up to the picnic table and informed Mama that he had done his fatherly duty.

We ate simple meals while we were on vacation; hamburgers, hot dogs, spaghetti, etc. One of our favorite meals was steamed clams. Danny and I oversaw digging the clams. We would each take a garden rake and a bucket down to the rocky beach and rake the rocks out of the way to find the clams. We would fill both of our buckets in a short time, take them up to the yard, wash them and put them in a large kettle of boiling water. They would steam until the shells would open. In the meantime, butter and garlic would be melting in another pan. When the clams were ready, we would start eating. All of us would gorge ourselves on steamed clams.

Another one of the teachers that Mama worked with had a cabin just a few houses down the shoreline from where we stayed. I remember being invited there for dinner one evening. We had spaghetti, salad, and homemade sourdough garlic bread. I was astounded at the spaghetti. Mrs. Kaufman had cooked the sauce all day. I had no idea what real spaghetti tasted like. Daddy only liked the kind from a box. I think he changed his mind after eating Mrs. Kaufman's spaghetti. We were all glad that we had to walk home. We had eaten a lot!

Even though life was somewhat strained being around Daddy so much, until Danny's death, I never remember him saying a negative word about his dad.

And Life Does Continue.

CHAPTER 15

From Danny to Dan

Dan Cottingham

Danton Thomas Cottingham was my brother. We were 4 days less than a year apart. My Birthday was on the 19th of October and his on the 23rd of October, one year earlier. We were very close and can honestly say that we only had one fight.

Everyone called him Danny until he was 13. Then he informed the family that he would not answer to Danny anymore, that he would be called Dan. I would slip sometimes and call him Danny, but he was always kind in his reminder to me to call him Dan. He was my best friend growing up; my playmate, my confidant and sometimes my partner in mischief although he was not happy about some of the situations I would present.

Dan was overweight during his middle and high school years and was very self-conscious about it. He did not get a lot of exercise during those years, and he did eat a lot.

When Dan was in the 8th grade, Mama enrolled him in a ballroom dancing class hoping that it would give him some confidence in himself. After his class he would come home and practice on me and teach me all the dance steps. Before we had TV, one of our favorite family activities was to dance. Daddy would put a stack of 45 RPM records on the player and we would dance. Mama and Daddy would dance, and Dan and I would dance. Then we would switch partners. During high school, Dan would often ask me to go to the dances with him because we could dance together so well.

Dan played the trombone in the high school band. He was large and getting taller all the time and when the band ordered new uniforms, they had to special order one for him. He really blossomed when he played the trombone. He was a very good musician and sat second chair for three years.

When Dan was 15, our dad died. 8 months later, our grandfather died. Both key men in his life were gone and we depended on each other even more.

After graduation from High School, Dan went to Portland State for one semester, but wasn't happy going to school. He had no idea what he wanted to do with his life. He got a job in a door factory for a while, but it did not last long. He sat around the house until Mama gave him an ultimatum—either enroll in school again, get a full-time job or join the military. He surprised us all by joining the Navy.

He spent 12 years in the Navy, including two tours in Vietnam, one unexpected trip to North Korean waters, and was assigned at various times to the USS Constellation, USS Enterprise, USS Truxton, and the USS Henry B. Wilson. He was stationed in San Diego, CA., Bremerton, WA., Norfolk, VA., Groton, CN., Arco, ID., and Camden, NJ.

In 1968, Dan married Billie. After his second tour in Vietnam, he realized that he had most of his sea duty still ahead of him and he would be gone from home a lot, so he and Billie decided to leave the Navy. During his time in service, he was assigned to nuclear powered ships and

LIFE AND LOVE CONTINUE

had extensive training at the Nuclear Training Center in Arco, Idaho. When he left the service, he was offered a job with Portland General Electric at the new Trojan Nuclear Power Plant on the Columbia River near Rainier, Oregon. He worked there until November 1984 when he was diagnosed with an inoperable brain tumor. He died in April 1986.

No matter where Dan was in the world, I was always able to rely on him, to trust him with my deepest feelings and to know unconditional love from him and to get it in return. I miss him every day.

"Pumpkin Pie"

One of Dan's favorite foods was Pumpkin Pie. He loved all pumpkin pies, but homemade was the best and his Nanama's recipe was special.

When Dan came from the East Coast to the West Coast on board the USS Truxton, he docked at the Long Beach Naval Station. We lived in Harbor City, not far from his base. We went to the base and brought him home to our house for a home cooked meal. I decided to be a nice sister and bake him a pumpkin pie. When we got home, he was so hungry that he ate most of the pie. After the first slice, I asked him how it tasted and he said that it was great, but not quite as sweet as he remembered. I tasted a bit and realized I had forgotten to add the sugar. I just added more sugar to the whipping cream, and he ate it anyway.

It was so much fun having him around. We picked him up whenever he could get the time off. Alan was taking a course at UCLA on Thursday evenings, so Patrick and I would pick Dan up at the base, bring him home to spend the evening with the baby and me, then Alan would take him back to the ship when he got home. It was good to spend so much time with him.

Our neighbor had a 2-year-old daughter, Tina. Tina had cerebral palsy and was subject to seizures. She was non-verbal and spastic. One weekend when Dan was there, Nita came running over with Tina in her arms crying that she was not breathing and was having a seizure. Dan immediately took her and administered CPR and got her breathing again. He held her and talked to her very quietly and she went to sleep in his arms. Nita said that she had never done that before with a stranger. After that, Dan was her new best friend. He received a commendation from the Navy for his actions in saving Tina. He was very humble about it, but we were so proud of him.

By the way, I never forgot the sugar in a pumpkin pie again.

No matter the sorrow of the loss of a loved one, Life Continues.

CHAPTER 16

Voyle Oliver Brunner (Buppa)

Voyle was "Buppa" to Danny and me. All our friends knew him as Buppa. When I was little and people would talk about Voyle or Grandpa, I had no idea who they were talking about, but the minute they said Buppa, I knew.

Buppa was not a large man, but he could do almost anything—build things, repair almost anything, garden and grow food, make great peanut butter and jelly sandwiches, wiggle his ears and he could draw. He drew all kinds of pictures, but the ones I liked best were the ones that went with the story he told me about "Spotty the Leopard". He made up the story as he went along and would draw pictures of Spotty's adventures or misadventures. Sadly, the stories were never written down and I do not know what happened to the pictures. I have not seen them since he drew them.

When we would go to a restaurant to eat, he always liked to sit in the back with his face to the front of the restaurant. He would pull out the small sketch pad he would carry in his shirt pocket and sketch faces, heads, hands—anything that he thought was unusual and unique. He liked to sketch old men and women's facial expressions.

Buppa was bald with only a fringe of hair around the lower part of his head. He was very proud of his bald head and told Danny and me that if we looked hard enough, we could see his brain.

On April 12, 1945, Daddy, Mama, Danny, and I were driving to Nanama and Buppa's house. It was Buppa's birthday, and we were going to have a party. Birthdays were special in our family, especially during the war years. Nanama would save up her sugar ration stamps and make a special birthday cake. She made the best cakes ever.

When we arrived at their house, both were standing on the front porch crying. They told Mama and Daddy that President Roosevelt had just died. Danny and I were too young to know what was going on. All we were concerned about was the cake and whether we would have a party or not. We did have a party, but all the adults were sad.

Between 1948 and 1952, Danny and I lived with our grandparents during the Summer and from January 1953 until June 1953, I lived with them because I was very sick, and they took care of me.

During the time I lived with them, my grandfather sexually molested me. It happened almost every night or early morning. When I was little, I thought it was normal and didn't think anything was wrong. I believed everything he told me, and he said that I should not tell anyone because they could not be included in the fun. It was because I believed him that I didn't say anything. It wasn't until after his death in 1957 that I could breathe easy and talk about it. I never did tell my mother. She adored her dad, and it would have hurt her too much. But what he did to me has affected me for the rest of my

LIFE AND LOVE CONTINUE

life. Some might wonder why I have written such negative things about my grandfather, but they are my memories whether good or bad. These just happened to be the bad ones.

He died on April 12, 1957, on his birthday. He was 72 years old.

No matter how difficult, Life Continues.

CHAPTER 17

The House at 3369 S. E. Schiller

The Tom Cottingham family lived at 4306 S. E. Ramona in Portland from 1943 until 1955. The house was a nice older home, but not really a home that was easy to entertain in. Tom, being the up-and-coming educator and future college professor, knew that he would have to do some serious entertaining. So, in 1954, he and Mama bought a lot, chose a house plan that would fit their needs, had it modified to fit the lot, hired a contractor, and proceeded to have a new house built. Because the general contractor under bid on the job, he tried to cut corners on some of the materials. Mama had specified in the final plans specific woods that she wanted for the cupboards and the floor. Because of her vigilance and daily visits to the sight, she got the house she wanted.

LIFE AND LOVE CONTINUE

Two days before Christmas, 1955, we moved into the house. We were all set for happy times in our new home. Not to be!! On September 1, 1956, Daddy died. It was just Mama, Dan, and me until April 1957. Buppa died on April 12th and Nanama came to live with us on that day. We knew that she would not be able to live by herself. Although she mourned Buppa for the rest of her life, she was always a joy to have around and was never a burden to any of us. She was not in good health, but the one job she could do to help around the house was to clean up the kitchen after dinner. Our kitchen was arranged so that she could move the dishes from the table onto a counter between the table and the sink, then she could walk around the counter and put the dishes into the dishwasher or sink. It saved her steps and the danger of falling with a handful of dirty plates.

I remember once when I had a friend over for dinner that she was horrified that we just got up and left the table after the meal was over. I explained to her about how my Nanama helped with the cleanup and that it was the only household chore that she felt able to do. My friend then understood why we left the table the way we did.

After I left college and started working, I had days off in the middle of the week. I would often call Nanama and tell her to put her coat and hat on, that we were going on an excursion. I would leave Mama a note that I had kidnapped Nanama for the day and we would take off. Sometimes we would go to the beach, sometimes to the mountains, but most of all, we would drive up to Multnomah Falls. It was always a nostalgic trip for us to go to the Falls.

When Mama was growing up, Buppa used to say that he and Nanama could hide anything from her underneath the dish pan. She would never find it because she hated to do dishes so much. When Mama and Daddy had the new house built, Daddy decided that an automatic dishwasher was not necessary. Mama and I could wash the dishes for a lot less money. After Daddy died, she had a dishwasher put in. Buppa lived long enough to see that dishwasher.

In August of 1957, Mama met John Talbott. They dated, fell in love, got engaged and were married on December 26, 1957. John was 15 years older than Mama, was a widower and had a grown, married son.

After a honeymoon to Arcata, CA to meet John's son Bob and his wife Shirley. John moved into the new home that was the dream home of his new wife and her deceased husband. Now picture: John had three brothers, no sisters, had 1 wife who died a year before, had no daughters and was not wise in the ways of teenage girls. He lived during the depression when extra money was non-existent, so spending for anything that was not an absolute necessity, was something he was not used to. On top of all that, he was not working at the time. He had a seasonal job in the lumber mills as a saw filer. Mama continued to teach school. He also had a new mother-in-law living in the household. Well, he moved in and within a few days, he was taking care of all of us. There were a few glitches along the way, but we worked them out and we quickly became one family. John, his son and daughter-in-law and extended family were the best thing that ever happened to us.

Mama was always an artist, drawing, painting, sewing, crocheting, knitting, and doing all kinds of needlecraft work. After John died in 1981, she started taking oil painting classes. She took the classes up until the year before her death and she did some incredible work. She painted a picture for each of her grandchildren and they are treasured possessions of each of them. She had prints made of most of her original paintings so that the kids could have those as well. She also did some beautiful decorative painting on wood and metal. Every time I decorate my home for the Holidays, I think of her. It is so special to have her beautiful artwork.

The joys of life continue.

CHAPTER 18

The Courtship of John Talbott And Mary Alice Cottingham

With the death of Daddy and Buppa, then Nanama coming to live with us, it was up to Mama to clean out her parents' home and get it ready to sell. My Grandparents had lived in their house for 20 years and had an accumulation of 43 years of stuff in the house. They were not prone to discard much of anything after doing without for so many years.

Mama had to wait until school was out to start the process of going through and either discarding, or distributing their belongings to the rest of the family. It was truly a daunting task for her. She was still mourning the death of her husband and father. Fortunately, she had just had the basement of our house finished and we had a place for a lot of the furniture. Some of the dishes, glassware and furniture were quite valuable.

Nanama had many canning jars and Mama did not want them. She had a friend who might want them. Pearl did a lot of canning. Pearl's brother-in-law was visiting them at the time. He had lost his wife the previous year also. Pearl thought that John would help Mama pack up the jars and take them to her house. After all the jars were in John's car, he mentioned that there was a movie that he wanted to see and asked if Mama would like to go with him. After that first date, things started happening, they dated until he went to Idaho for a job. Mama went to visit him at Thanksgiving, he proposed, bought her a ring, and drove her home after his job closed. They were married on December 26, 1957.

The meeting and marriage of John and Mary Alice was truly a blessing. He and his family were much loved.

John was an incredible man. He was raised on a farm in Missouri with his three brothers. He only finished the eighth grade and didn't have a lot of social graces, but was one of the smartest men I had ever known. He read the newspaper every day and was up on all of the latest news. He always had a book that he was reading. He was a very talented carpenter and could make just about anything out of wood. He built some beautiful furniture, built a house on the Oregon Coast, and took a 50-year-old house and completely remodeled it. When he and Mama moved in and he was landscaping the yard, he put up a tall flag pole on the street side of the property. Every morning, he would raise the flag and every evening he would lower it. One of his neighbors was a retired Army officer and was so impressed that John would go through that ritual every day. John had never served in the military, but he believed in honoring his country and its flag.

That bright red house became Grandma and Grandpa's house to all of their grandchildren.

John could grow just about anything. He always had a garden, growing corn and raspberries. His roses were prized all around the neighborhood and the nurses in his doctor's office loved it when he came in for an appointment. He always brought a bouquet of roses when they were in bloom.

In the early 1970's, John had hip replacement surgery. At that time, the surgery could be complicated and John was laid up for quite a while. After he was healed, he had one leg that was several inches shorter than the other and had to have a special shoe made to accommodate his gait and balance. When John was helping me plant my garden one Spring, he would put a plant in the ground, cover it with soil and tamp it down with his large shoe. Then he would point his finger at the plant and say, "Now you grow!" The plant always obeyed. He had the magic touch with growing gardens. We certainly always enjoyed the fruits of his labors.

John was a saw-filer in a lumber mill. He worked hard all day, but would come home and take care of his garden in the evening.

John and Mama had a camper that they put on the back of their pickup and after John retired in 1965, they spent their summers traveling. After Mama retired in 1977, they sold the camper and graduated to a travel trailer.

John died in 1981 and I still miss his unique sayings and his wisdom.

And the love of life continues.

John and Bob Talbott	John Talbott

CHAPTER 19

Life after High School

In 1959, I graduated from high school and started working at Sears, Roebuck in the young girl's department. I worked during the summer and over the Christmas Holidays. I loved working in the girl's department. It was fun helping the young girls pick out clothes for school. Many times, their taste and their mother's taste clashed, and I would try to come up with an alternative that both of them liked. I worked next to the infant's department. That was my downfall. In August 1959, my niece Sherrie Talbott was born and most of my paycheck went for baby clothes.

In September, I started college at Lewis and Clark College in Portland. Because my father had been a professor there, I was given free tuition. Because of the tuition break, I was able to afford to live on campus. I started out with two roommates and boy, were we crammed in there. It was a small room with a single bed and a bunk bed. I had never had to share a room before, so it was quite an adjustment for me. When the roommates got into my things, borrowed without asking and wearing my clothes because they did not have any clean ones, I got mad. We eventually worked our differences, but it continued to be tense.

One of my roommates and another girl that lived in the same dorm, were from Santa Barbara, California. During Spring Break, we decided to drive to Santa Barbara to visit their parents. Four of us decided to go and we had a ball. We drove down to California, thru San Francisco and down Hwy 101 to Santa Barbara. We had so much fun seeing the sights. I had never been on the coast of California before, so San Francisco, Monterey and Carmel and Big Sur were all new to me. We toured Hearst Castle and probably, like any young girl, it transported me back to that time. I do not have too much recollection of Santa Barbara itself. We were only there a couple of days as we had to get back to Portland and classes. But I have great memories of the trip down the coast road.

I went to college for 2 years but quit after the second year. My grades went down, and I was suffering emotionally from the stress. I had quite a bit of pressure from some of my professors who knew my father. They expected me to do great work because my dad was so smart. I thought I would transfer to another school in the State but realized that my dad had connections in all of the State run schools. It was likely that I would come against the same problem as he was a guest lecturer at most of the state schools in the Western part of Oregon.

After long discussions with my mother, she suggested that I quit school for a while. I was shocked that she suggested it, but pleased that she understood the problems that I was having.

So, in June of 1961, I was looking for a full-time job. I was not having much success when Sears called to see if I would work during the Summer. When I told them that I needed to find a full-time job as I was no longer in school, they suggested that I come in and apply there for full-time work. I did apply and was hired the same day. I went to work in the Customer Service Department. I started out taking in items to be repaired or replaced. Sears had a "Satisfaction Guaranteed or your Money Back" policy and some customers really took advantage of it. One customer brought in an old rusty crescent wrench. He told us that he was not satisfied with the wrench, and he wanted his money back. He also told me that he dug the wrench up out of his garden. Sears stood behind their motto and gave him his money back.

Some small appliances were sent back to the manufacturer for a decision on repairing or replacing. We sent a toaster back for repair and heard that it did not work because there was a dead mouse in the bottom of it. The customer received a brand new toaster in return. Sears stood behind their motto.

I was eventually transferred to the package pickup area. Customers shopping in the store could have their purchases sent to the package pickup and get all of them at one time. During Christmas and back to school seasons, I was always busy. Customers were lined up outside the door.

One of the very important jobs I had was to make sure the cash register receipts were totaled and balanced every day. There was one day when it would not balance, and I was a little over one dollar off. Boy was I nervous. It was the first time that I was not balanced perfectly. The next day, the Superintendent of the store, the Personnel Director and my immediate boss, the Customer Service Manager were wandering around the loading dock area where my office was. They talked to several of the warehousemen and occasionally glanced into my office and the pickup area. I was very nervous because of the shortage in the till the day before. The next day I was called into the conference room where all three of the men sat. I felt like I was being sent to the gallows. Well, I was not fired, but offered a job in the personnel department as head of the new employee training. I was so relieved that I still had a job and would be working away from the cold loading dock.

After working for two years, I bought a car—a 1961 VW Bug for $600.00. That was the largest purchase I had ever made, but I loved having a car of my own. No more taking the bus or depending on others to get me to work.

Now that I had a car, I thought it was time for an apartment of my own. Mama suggested that I look for a reliable roommate to share expenses. I had enough furniture and stuff to fill two apartments as my grandmothers' things were still packed and stored in our basement. I found a roommate and an apartment, and we moved in right away. The apartment was only about 10 minutes from work. With help from the 10% employee discount at Sears, I was able to purchase the rest of the things that we needed.

Carla was my roommate for about a year until she got married and moved out of the area.

Carla and I took our first paid vacation together to San Francisco. We started out driving about 9:00 P.M on a Friday evening after attending a co-workers wedding. Interstate 5 was still under construction and the route South was a mess. It was treacherous after dark. At one point, Carla was outside walking beside the car with her hand on the fender so that we could stay on the road. Oh, did I mention that we were driving in pea soup fog. Thank goodness there was very little traffic. We stopped in Medford for gas and to rest awhile. After about 3 hours of sleep in the car, we drove on to San Francisco.

We drove into the city and found our hotel, parked the car, and went on our merry way by foot or bus. We saw all the sights of the city and had such a good time. We either walked or took the bus to see Chinatown, Fishermen's Wharf, Beacon Hill, all the fancy homes on Nob Hill and Golden Gate Park. When we drove home, we drove across the Golden Gate and made sure that we hit I-5 during the daylight hours. We were very proud that we had a successful first vacation.

The next year, I took another vacation with two other girls. We went camping at Lake Tahoe. I had my first introduction to slot machines while there. I put a nickel in a machine and pulled the handle. Suddenly bells and whistles went off. I thought I had broken the machine, but I had won $7.50. I thought I was rich. We had a great time visiting the casinos at Reno and Lake Tahoe. It was another memorable vacation.

In 1964, Dan was stationed at the Naval Nuclear Training Center in Arco, Idaho. In March he called and asked if Mama and I could come for a visit. It was Mama's Spring break, so we piled into Mama's Red Ford Falcon Station Wagon and took off for Idaho Falls, the nearest town to Arco, where Dan lived. It was the first time that just the two of us had gone on a trip together. We had so much fun together, laughing and singing songs and Mama told stories about her high school days. The only problem was that Mama was a heavy snorer and I did not get very much sleep. I did sleep in the car while she was driving.

We arrived at Dan's motel room (he lived in a motel with long term housing). It had been a while since we had seen him, so we had a lot to catch up on. He had Thursday, Friday, and Saturday off. On

Thursday, his unit had a big family picnic and softball game. It was the first time that Dan had ever had family at one of the unit's get together. It was good to meet the other people that he worked with and their families.

On Friday, Dan suggested that we go to Yellowstone National Park. He assured us that it was not very far, so off we went. Neither Mama nor I had ever been there before, so we were excited to see it. After a pretty drive, we entered the park and were awed by everything we saw, especially the buffalo. Neither of us had ever seen one before. We finally made it to Old Faithful. The geyser had just gone off, so we had about an hour to wait. There were a few wooden benches to sit on, but not many other amenities. As we were waiting there, Dan laid down on one of the benches and went to sleep. When he awoke, he said that it was funny that all these people would wait for a stream of hot water to come out of the ground for a few seconds, and then wait for another hour to see it all over again. Everyone started to laugh and agreed with him. It was a beautiful day, and we enjoyed seeing all of the sights. After we left the park, we stopped for supper then headed West, back to Idaho Falls. At one point, I was driving and it was very dark. There were no other cars on the road and only my headlights to see by. It seemed no one else was on the road. Suddenly, a large elk leaped across the road in front of the car. I slammed on the brakes causing Dan to slide off the back seat and Mama to pitch forward. Fortunately, the elk did not hit the windshield. I was too nervous to drive anymore, so Dan drove the rest of the way home.

Dan had arranged for a tour of the nuclear plant where he was training. This was before there were restrictions on entering the facilities. Of course, there were some areas that we were not allowed to see, but it was fascinating to hear them talk about their work, even though I did not understand most of it. Dan spent about 5 years there, teaching after his training was finished.

We left Idaho Falls on Saturday afternoon to get home in time for work on Monday morning. It was a great week and so good to spend time with Dan.

LIFE AND LOVE CONTINUE

I worked for Sears for five years when the travel bug hit me again. In 1966, I went to both Alaska and Europe. When I returned from Europe, I went to work for Sears again, but in June 1967, I met the love of my life, quit my job at the end of August, got married and moved to Southern California.

And Love makes life continue.

CHAPTER 20

Aunt Dede

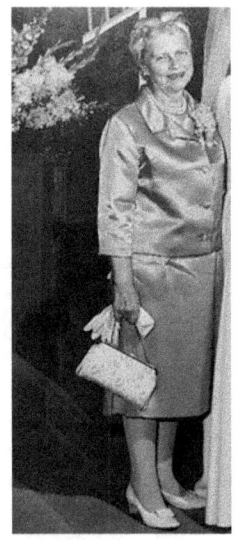

Aunt Dede

Laura Valeda Stuart was born March 19, 1897, the fourth daughter of William and Mary Stuart. At the time of her birth, her sister Alice had two children, so Laura was an aunt when she was born. She lived and worked in Riperia, WA at the family hotel, but soon moved to the Willamette Valley in Western Oregon. She lived mostly in the Salem and Portland areas. She met and married Art Berry in Salem and lived there most of their married life. They moved to Portland after his retirement.

LIFE AND LOVE CONTINUE

Because Laura, when a child, could not pronounce her name, she called herself Dede and that nickname stuck for the rest of her life, She and Art had no children, so she adopted her sister's children as hers and their grandchildren as her grandchildren. I was one of those privileged great-grandchildren.

Aunt Dede was the epitome of a great lady. She was impeccably groomed, and she always stood up straight, even though only 5'4" tall. Her home was spotless, but always felt welcoming to anyone who visited. When I was working at Sears, her home was close to mine, and I would often stop by for a chat. Her door was always open to me.

When I was planning my wedding, I tried to always include her in the plans. I would stop by to take her with me to pick out flowers or the cake or my going away outfit. On one of those trips, she handed me $500.00 to help with the expenses. I was so grateful. I was trying to pay for most of the wedding expenses myself and the extra money went a long way towards paying the bills.

In August 1968, Dan was getting married in Portland and we took our baby boy, Patrick home for the wedding. Aunt Dede was able to meet him and sit and cuddle him for a while. Sadly, she died on October 18, 1968. I do miss her sweet smile and our good chats.

Even in sadness, life continues.

CHAPTER 21

The Old Stuart Hotel

Riperia, Washington was a small town on the Snake River in Eastern Washington. It was at the end of the Camas Prairie railway line where the trains reversed and went back down the Snake and Columbia Rivers.

The William Stuart family owned the hotel in Riperia. The hotel was also the diner, the post office, the mayor's office, and the center of activity for the city. There was also a smokehouse and blacksmith shop in the back. It was the hub of the town where everyone met for the daily news.

By the early 1950's, Riperia was a ghost town. The trains had stopped running and the hotel was sold when Grandpa and Grandma Stuart died. In the early 1960's my Aunt Dede, who grew up there, found out that a dam was going to be built on the Snake River and would subsequently flood the whole area and Riperia would be under water. Aunt Dede and Uncle IO, two of the five children of William Stuart wanted to see the town before it was gone. Aunt Dede knew the people who had the key to the hotel.

So, in the Spring of 1964, Aunt Dede, Uncle IO, Mama, John, and I drove to Eastern Washington to visit Riperia. It was a fun trip and an educational one for me.

Aunt Dede got the keys to the hotel so we could see the inside. Aunt Dede and Uncle IO reminisced about their past and talked as if they were alone. They had lived in a house near the hotel so that all the rooms were available for paying customers. Because of the rail traffic, the rooms were almost always filled.

LIFE AND LOVE CONTINUE

Most of the houses were already gone, but Aunt Dede pointed out the house that Mama was born in. This was the first time she had been back to Riperia. We walked all over the area and had quite an education from the two former residents. We learned where the school was and where different friends lived. We learned about getting around in the winter and how hot it would get in the summer. The Snake river was a favorite place for the young people to congregate on a hot summer evening.

John rummaged around in the blacksmith shop and found a pair of horse hames, the part of a harness for a horse to pull a wagon. He took them home and made a beautiful chandelier for their dining room. I went home from that trip with a better insight of my heritage and how my ancestors lived.

It was fun seeing a part of my past and heritage thru the eyes of someone who grew up there.

And life goes on.

CHAPTER 22

Driving to Alaska

In 1966, Mama and John wanted to make a trip to Alaska to visit friends of ours. They lived in Anchorage on the campus of Alaska Methodist University. My parents planned to drive the Alcan Highway in their pickup and camper. They asked me if I wanted to go with them, So, I took a 3 week leave- of- absence and off we went.

The highway from Dawson Creek to the Alaska border was not paved. It was about 1400 miles of dust and dirt road. The driving was easy on the dirt road as it was well graded and when the weather cooperated, we could make fairly good time.

The only drawback was the dust. There was dust on everything outside and inside of the camper. Every evening when we stopped for the night, we had to clean the entire inside of the camper before we could even think about fixing a meal. We were lucky that we had followed a rainstorm most of the way, as it held the dust down, but it was still bad. We had large sheets of plastic covering the bed, sofa, and table inside the camper. All our cameras, purses, and personal items—toothbrushes, cosmetics, etc. were put under the plastic so that the dust would not destroy them. Whenever we stopped, John set the camper up, putting down the jacks and leveling them. Mama would fold the plastic and put things away so that we could sleep, and I washed the counters, stove, and table. I even had to wash the tops of the latches that opened and closed the cupboards.

It took us 7 days to drive from Dawson City, BC to Dawson Creek in the Yukon Territory, where we met our friends Alice and Chet. Dawson Creek was a gold rush town and famous as a gathering

LIFE AND LOVE CONTINUE

place for prospectors. There was a saloon on every corner, loud noises, and lots and lots of girls. After taking a walking tour of the city, visiting museums, and even attending the local Methodist Church, we tried panning for gold. No luck for any of us, but we had fun standing in a cold creek in our bare feet.

From Dawson City, we took a ferry across the Yukon River and into Alaska. Finally, some paved roads. But, the paved roads were worse than the unpaved ones in Canada. The perma-frost buckled the pavement and made the road very uneven and bumpy. Thus, we learned to appreciate the unpaved roads after a mile of driving on Alaska's paved ones.

Instead of driving directly to Anchorage, we took the road North to Eagle, Alaska. What a lovely little outpost on the Yukon River and marvelous people. When we discovered that the RV Park was full of mosquitos, the owners of the lodge and café offered their front yard for us to camp in. One of the owners of the lodge was also the postmistress, the café owner and cook, the assistant to the mayor and the local librarian. Her husband was the mayor and the local State Park Ranger. It was his job to take a water sample of the Yukon River every day and send it to the Capitol for analysis.

He invited us to ride along with him on one of his trips. We saw some wildlife that we might never have seen otherwise. The State of Alaska tested the viability of the water to see if it would sustain the Salmon migration. Apparently, it was unusual at the time for anyone to travel to the North side of the Yukon River in that area. We did not get off of the boat, but we saw a mama moose and her two babies, deer, several different waterfowl, a couple of bears, along with other creatures I cannot remember. It was a memorable boat ride.

While we were there, the rhubarb was ripe, and the cook made a rhubarb pie. Since her husband did not like rhubarb, the pie was cut into 6 pieces, and we reaped the rewards. She made one every day that we stayed there. We would purchase the whole pie and asked her to join us. It was some of the best rhubarb pie I had ever eaten, even my Grandma's. That is really saying a lot!

From Eagle, we drove to Anchorage. Poor John, we had to fill the pickup with gasoline and he was shocked to have to pay 50 cents a gallon for gasoline in Alaska. He installed two extra gas tanks onto the bed of the pickup before we left Portland, so we would have plenty of fuel in case we did not find stations along the way. But when he filled all three tanks, it was expensive. Oh, to be able to pay 50 cents a gallon now!

Alice and Chet lived in a duplex on the campus of the Alaska Methodist University. Mama and John stayed in the house with them, and I slept in the camper parked in their driveway. In July, there are almost 24 hours of daylight which made it hard to get to sleep. The house had blackout curtains, but the camper did not. One morning about 4:00, I woke up and looked outside into the face of a moose, looking inside at me. She must have been checking out this strange structure in her territory. It scared me to see her up so close and I'm sure I scared her.

Alice and Chet showed us where they were when the 1964 Earthquake hit. There was still a lot of evidence of the quake 2 years later. They happened to be downtown in the middle of all the destruction and were lucky to be able to get out unhurt.

A train trip to Fairbanks took us close to Denali and Mt. McKinley. It is rare to be able to see the mountain so clearly, but we did. And it was magnificent! We stayed overnight in Fairbanks and were able to visit Santa's village at North Pole, Alaska. Quite a tourist trap, but fun to visit.

After a few more days in Anchorage and a short trip to Hope, Alaska, and Portage Glacier, I boarded a plane to return to Portland. Mama and John stayed for another month. What a memorable trip that was.

And life and love go on.

CHAPTER 23

Judy's Adventures in Europe

In the Summer of 1966, I had been working for Sears for a little over 5 years. I was 24 years old, with no prospects for anything different in the near future. I worked with three women who were in their 40's and 50's, were never married, had no families and it seemed, only lived for their jobs. The thought of becoming like them was very scary to me. So, two of my girlfriends and I decided to go to Europe and possibly get jobs there. We started planning the trip in June and were planning to leave in October. We applied for our passports, purchased rail passes for both Europe and England, Scotland and Ireland and started saving every penny that we could.

In October, we boarded a train in Portland bound for Vancouver, BC to fly Canadian Airlines polar route to Amsterdam, Holland. When we arrived at our hotel in Vancouver, all three of us realized that we had way too much luggage, so we had to decided what to send back home and only have 1 suitcase each. Never having traveled much before, we had a hard time deciding what we would need. We finally sent 1 suitcase each home via UPS and off we went.

The flight we were on took us to Amsterdam, Holland and then the next day to London. Our first sight of Holland was all the red roofs on the houses. We took a taxi to our hotel, got settled a bit, then went out and did a little sightseeing, but we were tired from jet lag, so only wanted to sleep. We knew we would be back in Amsterdam later in the trip, so we tried to get rid of the jet lag so that we would be fresh and able to enjoy London.

The next day, we arrived at Heathrow Airport in London and took a taxi to our hotel. The ride was exciting and very scary. They drive on the left side of the road, and it was so hard to adjust to. Because our funds were limited, we stayed in a cheap hotel. It was very large and catered to young people. Breakfast was included in the rate, so we knew that we would at least have one meal a day. The first morning, I ordered a soft-boiled egg. The waitress pulled one out of her apron pocket and set it in an egg cup. I had never seen an egg cup before and had no idea how to eat the egg. I watched the other diners and finally figured out how to open the egg with my knife.

Our first order of business was to figure out the subway system. Taxis were too expensive and the subway was cheap. Once we figured out the map and where we wanted to go, we were all set to be tourists traveling on a budget. We also, when we could, took the bus, mostly sitting on the top deck so we could see the sights.

The British Museum was within walking distance of our hotel, so that was the first place we went. I had read about the Magna Carta and was awed at being able to see the actual document. During our few days in London, we saw all the usual sights, Changing of the Guard at Buckingham Palace, St. Paul's Cathedral where they pointed out the bomb damage during WWII, Big Ben, and Westminster Abbey.

We took a train to Runnymede and saw the piece of land that was given to the United States in honor of President Kennedy. Runnymede is also a memorial to the Allied forces during the war. We were able to travel to Hampton Court and tour the castle there. We took the train to Windsor Castle and took the tour of the castle. That was one of the highlights for me. We were disappointed that the Queen was not in residence at the time, but we had a great time touring her home. We were able to see the "Old Curiosity Shop" of Dickens fame and we toured the Tower of London and saw the crown jewels. We watched the ravens at the tower and the swans on the Thames River.

I turned 25 while we were in London. It was quite a milestone for me and always remember where I was and what I was doing on that birthday.

LIFE AND LOVE CONTINUE

Soon it was time to board a train and head North for Scotland. One of the girls I was traveling with had relatives in Duns, Scotland, a small town just across the border from England. We stayed there in a lovely little hotel and spent most of the day and evening with Lynn's family. We were served a proper "high tea" that was outstanding. There was enough food left over for supper that evening. Tea was served at 4 PM and supper at 7 PM. They also took us to a typical Scottish Pub and we had a great time singing, dancing, and drinking. We spent 2 days with them and they were the most loving and gracious hosts.

After 2 days, we boarded the train for Edinboro. I don't remember much about the city, except touring the castle. Edinboro castle is the Queen's residence when she is in Scotland and is a real fortress. It is sitting way up on a hill and is very large and old. It would be very hard for someone to "storm the castle."

We spent one night in Edinboro then took the train across the country to Glasgow. Unfortunately, I have no recognition of Glasgow at all. We did not spend a night there, but took the train South to Ayr, Scotland. Ayr is the birthplace of the poet, Robert Burns, who wrote the songs, "Auld Lang Syne" and "Flow Gently Sweet Afton". I was most excited about seeing the original verses and scores. We stayed in a little hotel in Ayr and decided to see a movie that evening. "Seven Brides for Seven Brothers" was showing at their theater, and even though we had seen it before, we thought it would be fun to see it again. It was a little ironic that the movie is based on 7 brothers who are loggers in Oregon. While in Ayr, I purchased a pretty tea set, (tea pot, coffee pot, creamer, and sugar bowl). The shop packed it for me and sent it home. It was my one souvenir from the entire trip.

From Ayr, we boarded the train for the trip back to Glasgow, Edinboro and then back to London. We stayed in the same hotel because it was cheap. The hotel had a large bar that we frequented often. We would play 3 handed pinochle, which was a totally foreign game to the British. We were having a beer and playing cards one afternoon when 3 lorry (truck) drivers came up to us and asked if they could buy us another beer. Of course, we said yes. One of the fellows picked up the cards and started doing some card tricks. He was getting very frustrated because his tricks were not working and he was falling flat on impressing us. He did not know that a pinochle deck only has 48 cards in it. They were very nice, polite young men and asked to take us to dinner. We went to an Indonesian Restaurant. WOW—Hot food! And the beer in England was not cold. Super-hot food and warm beer was not the best combination. We did have a nice evening and were impressed by how polite the guys were.

The next day, we got on the train and went to Dover to board the ferry to cross the English Channel. So far, the weather had been very good, cold but no rain. Well, the weather going across the channel was terrible. It was stormy and there were high waves. I was okay if I stayed on deck and had fresh air, but the minute I went below, I started to get sick. So, I froze all the way across the channel. It was fun to look back to England and see the White Cliffs of Dover though. I did not know that they were real. I thought that it was just a song title. I was impressed.

The ferry took us from Dover to Pas- De- Calais, France. My first impression of Calais was that it was very dark and dirty. We stayed in a small hotel with a communal bathroom down the hall and only a bidet in the room. I had never seen a bidet before. We only stayed one night there and boarded the train the next day for Lyon, France and then Brussels, Belgium. In Brussels, we checked into our hotel and right away took a walking tour of the Grand-Place, the central square in Brussels. We saw the NATO Buildings and the Atomium, originally built for the 1958 World's Fair.

We had booked a tour of Waterloo ahead of time and boarded the bus for the tour. I do not remember much about Waterloo but do remember the 3 soldiers we met on the bus. They were on leave from a base in Germany. They took us to dinner that evening, and we had more than enough to drink. We ended up walking down the main street of Brussels arm in arm, singing "Dixie". When we got back to our hotel, we were locked out. We did not know that there was a curfew. We spent the night in the lobby of their hotel. We got back to our hotel at 6 AM, packed up and got on the train for Holland.

We stopped in The Hague and Rotterdam and then went into Amsterdam. We took a walking tour of the city, went to the

Rijksmuseum, and saw Rembrandt's "The Night Watch"—very impressive. We toured the Ann Frank house and climbed the hidden stairs and went into the rooms where she wrote her diaries. We took a boat trip along he canals and saw the 7 bridges then went out into the harbor. We toured the Van Gogh Museum and saw some of his most famous works, especially his self-portrait.

    I knew that I was running out of money and would not be able to continue with the trip as planned. I let the others know that I was heading home. Before we left Portland, I had the good sense to leave my return fare with my parents. I notified them that I was coming home and to wire the money to me via the American Express Office in Amsterdam. I walked about three miles to the American Express office every day to see if the money was there. I was not eating. I couldn't afford to. I had $3.00 to my name and did not know how I was going to pay my hotel bill. The hotel was a bed and breakfast, so I had coffee every morning and some rolls. I would take the rest of the rolls and stuff them in my purse. That is what I would eat for the rest of the day. One of the days when I was walking, I passed out on the street. God was certainly with me that day because I passed out right in front of the hospital. After I was fed in the hospital, they put me on a bus to the American Embassy where I called my parents to see if they had wired the money. They had and someone at the Express office had put the notice in the wrong area. I was able to get the money, book a flight to New York City and JFK Airport via Lufthansa Airline and take a taxi to a restaurant and have dinner. I had dinner at a Chinese restaurant in the red-light district. It was the safest place for a single lady to be. Prostitution was highly regulated in The Netherlands and the ladies were all sitting behind windows and not walking the streets.

    The next morning, I paid my hotel bill, took a taxi to the train station, and boarded the train for Luxembourg and the plane for home. After a nine-hour (very crowded) flight, we landed at JFK Airport. I took a taxi to Grand Central Station and bought a train ticket to Portland. The taxi driver was very nice and pointed out a lot of the sights of New York, while he was driving me to Grand Central Station. I spent the whole day in the station and finally boarded the train to Chicago where I changed stations and trains, then headed home. The train took the highline route across the country and I was able to see some beautiful areas of the United States that I had not seen before. Even though I was not feeling well and anxious to get home, I did enjoy the train trip. Unfortunately, I took my shoes off at the beginning of the trip and my feet and ankles swelled so badly that I could not get me shoes back on. I departed the train in Portland with my slippers on.

It was good to be home and remember the fun times and good memories.

But life does go on.

CHAPTER 24

Bus trip to New Jersey

I came back from my trip to Europe in November and moved in with Mama and John, was rehired at Sears and rode the bus to and from work. Life was not very exciting, but I was starting over.

Since I sold my VW Bug to help finance my trip to Europe, when I returned home the only transportation I had was the city bus.

Dan was stationed in Camden, New Jersey and was assigned to the U.S.S. Truxton, a support ship for the aircraft carrier the USS Enterprise which was preparing to sail around the Horn of South America and along the Pacific coast to Long Beach, Ca.

Dan had a 1964 Corvair Convertible, black with red interior—that he did not want to sell, so he called to make me a deal, come to Camden in four days and he would let me use the car while he was at sea. I jumped at the chance to use that car. I let Mama and John know of my plans and that I would be going by Greyhound bus to pick the car up and drive it home. They were concerned about me going by myself, so John offered to go with me and help me drive home. John was 66 years old, had just retired the year before, had severe asthma and arthritis and would have to sit for four days on the bus, but he was ready to go. He had never been further East than Missouri and was eager to see the area.

It was a long four days, and we were both sore by the time we arrived in Philadelphia. Dan met us there, showed us some of the sights of the city, then took us across the water to Camden. We met some of his good friends, had a very nice dinner with them, checked into our hotel and had a good night's sleep.

The next morning, we loaded up the car and headed West. Dan was concerned about the tires, so he put three extra ones in the trunk. We planned our route home but made the mistake of getting on the Pennsylvania Turnpike. We were at the mercy of Howard Johnson's restaurants and Gulf Service Stations. The only bright spot was that John was able to have a catfish dinner at the Howard Johnson's restaurant, which he loved. We were on the turnpike until Pittsburg, paid an enormous toll, and stayed off of that highway for the rest of the trip through Pennsylvania.

We traveled through Ohio, Michigan, Iowa, Nebraska and on West. We stopped at a rest stop with a hickory grove and John got very excited because he had hickory trees on his farm in Missouri. We also found a town in Nebraska where he had some relatives buried, so he had a chance to visit the graves and take some pictures. The newly planted corn fields of Nebraska were impressive in their size. The Great Plains were so flat, and the Rockies were so high. We continued through Wyoming and Idaho and into Oregon. We saw the end of our trip ahead. The car performed well, but we were still worried about the tires. We bought a new tire in Pennsylvania, and all was well until we reached Oregon. Driving from Ontario, Oregon to La Grande, Oregon, we had a blow-out, causing a hole in the muffler. We changed the tire, but there was nothing we could do about the noise of the muffler until we got to Portland. On the hill between LaGrande and Pendleton we were stopped by a State Patrolman for making excessive noise. We gave him the sad story of the blow-out and the hole in the muffler. He was very nice and gave me a warning to show, if I should get stopped again. We went directly to a repair shop when we reached Portland and had it fixed.

I enjoyed driving that car and I thanked Dan many times over for lending it to me. Then, bless his heart, he signed it over to Alan and me as a wedding present in September 1967.

We drove that car to California when we moved there and I drove it up until Patrick was born. We had to park the car on the street in front of our apartment in Harbor City, California and 24 hours after Patrick was born, a drunken sailor turned the corner too fast and plowed into it. The car was repaired, but never ran the same. We were very sorry to see it go.

And Life and Fun Continue.

CHAPTER 25

The Meeting, Courtship and Marriage of Alan Perkins and Judy Cottingham

I met Alan on June 17, 1967, on a blind date arranged by a co-worker of mine. I was living with my parents and had no one special in my life at the time.

It was a Saturday evening, and I was in bed by 8:30 PM. At 9:00 PM, the phone rang for me. It was a guy named Alan Perkins saying that my name was given to him by my co-worker. He asked me if I

LIFE AND LOVE CONTINUE

would like to go to a fraternity party. At that point in my life, I was game for anything. I gave him directions to the house.

He arrived in about 40 minutes. Thinking we would leave right away, I was ready to walk out the door, but he came in, shook my parents' hands, and sat down to talk to them. He explained his college history, his time in the Army, about his severe auto accident, his religion, and his fraternal affiliations. My parents were very impressed with how polite he was and his determination to finish college.

We finally left and went to a fraternity brothers' home for a swimming pool party. We left after about 2 hours and went to a lounge and went dancing. We danced until our feet were about ready to fall off. During one of the dances, Alan asked, "will you marry me?" I told him he didn't know me well enough. We left, drove to my parents, and sat in the car in the driveway and talked about our individual dreams, learning about families and our history. After some daytime sleep, Alan returned for another date and asked me again to marry him. This time I said "yes". Because Alan was being transferred to Southern California in August, a hastily planned wedding was in order.

We chose September 9th as our wedding day and proceeded with the plans. We both decided that we wanted a good-sized wedding. We were both very involved in fraternal organizations, work and families and had lots of friends and family to invite. In the meantime, we had a busy summer, meeting friends, family and getting to know each other.

Mama was busy making my wedding dress. She put three different patterns together and designed the dress around those patterns. She put so much love into that dress. It was beautiful work of art.

Alan left for El Segundo, CA the 3rd week in August. He drove his car down there and would fly home, then we would drive my car down after the wedding. He found us a place to live in Redondo Beach, California. He flew home a week before the wedding. My brother Dan also came home on leave at the same time.

Billie, a bridesmaid, had met Dan before and they had not clicked, so she was apprehensive about doing anything with him. I had to get her long white gloves and we met at a lounge in the shopping center mall. I had asked Billie if she would mind if Dan came along. And she said that would be okay, but she could not stay very long. We all had a drink then Billie and I went to get her gloves and returned for another drink with the fellows. She was having a good time talking to Dan and decided that she would go out to dinner with us. Things seemed to click for them that evening and they were pretty much inseparable while he was home on leave. They became engaged while he was home and were married the next year.

Our wedding was magical. A woman from the church sang two songs, "Whither Thou Goest" and "Oh Perfect Love". Both Alan and I spoke up and made no mistakes while saying our vows. We were making a vow to our families, to ourselves, to each other and to God. Our future was set with those vows.

After the wedding, we went on a short honeymoon to Southern Oregon and the coast, then returned to Portland to get ready for the move to Redondo Beach. The moving van came to pack all our stuff. It was all in Mama's basement and I'm sure she was very glad to get rid of it and have her basement back. Since Alan drove his car down to California, we took my car on the trip South. We turned the drive South into an extended honeymoon. The coast road was our route of choice. We went to the Redwood National Forest in Northern California. I had never been there before, and it was beautiful. We continued South to Monterey to the Jazz Festival. It was okay, but I have never been one for jazz music. It was fun seeing the city of Monterey though. From there we drove thru Carmel which is full of beautiful homes and then on to Big Sur. Holy Cow that was beautiful, but the road was scary to me. Especially since I was sitting on the Ocean side of the car and the cliffs were so high and really a long way down. They were also very curvy. A tour of Hearst Castle gave us a view into the life of the rich and famous. I had been there before, but saw it from a different perspective with Alan beside me. On we drove, to Santa Barbara and Oxnard and then into Los Angeles.

LIFE AND LOVE CONTINUE

Alan had rented us a cute little house in Redondo Beach about two blocks from the beach and the Ocean. It was the back house on the lot. A young couple with a 2-year-old baby lived in the front house.

Our married life started in that little house. We had so much fun getting to know and entertaining our new neighbors.

We decided to fix a Thanksgiving dinner for ourselves with all the trimmings. I had fixed holiday meals many times before and felt confident that I could pull off a tasty meal. I was making Cranberry relish in the blender. The cranberries were being chopped and I was getting ready to put the orange rind and sugar in when Alan came home from work and decided that he would open the lid of the blender and stir the cranberries. The only problem was that he forgot to turn the blender off. Cranberries were everywhere—all over his dress shirt and suit pants the counter and cupboards and even the ceiling. When we finished cleaning up and finished making the relish, what was left tasted pretty good. We have laughed about that ever since.

My brother Dan was able to visit several times from the Long Beach Naval Station.

Our biggest joy during that time was watching my stomach grow with the baby that was going to come into our lives. We lived in the house for several months when we realized that we would need something less expensive. We found an apartment in a large complex in Harbor City. We moved in and awaited the birth of our baby. On May 2, 1968, Patrick Alan Perkins was born. He weighed a little over 6 lbs. and was the most beautiful baby ever born. We were filled with joy and awe when we looked at him.

Alan started taking some classes at UCLA, working towards completing his bachelor's degree. He only had a few hours left to finish. He went to class on Thursday evenings, and I was able to get Dan from the Naval Base and he spent the evening with Patrick and me. Also, about that time I decided that I needed to go back to work. I found a babysitter who would take care of Pat in her home. She lived in Hawthorne, CA and there was an apartment available next door to her, so we moved again. We thought it would be an ideal situation. She was married and had a baby about the same time that Patrick was born. It so happened that we went to High School together in Portland, so I was very comfortable leaving Patrick with her. Unfortunately, it did not work out so well. I was home one day when the doorbell rang, and a lady said she was looking for Carole. She mentioned that she certainly enjoyed having Patrick at her home every day and that he was such a good baby to take care of. I was shocked. Come to find out, Carole was taking Patrick to this lady's home for her to watch him while she was at home taking care of her own child. Fortunately, the lady was very nice and apologized to me on Carole's behalf. Carole did not babysit again. I changed my work schedule to part-time in the evening so that Alan was home to take care of Patrick.

In August of 1969, Alan found out that he had to finish his degree on campus at Portland State University. He was in jeopardy of losing some of the credits that he had already earned. We were living in Southern California every day with news of murders, theft, rioting and general disorderly conduct by citizens. It was not a safe place to raise a family. Because of the tension and the fact that Alan had to finish school on Campus, we made the decision to move back to Portland about the first of September.

Mama found us a duplex that we could afford, and John flew down to help us drive a U-Haul back to Portland. When he got off the plane in Los Angeles, he had a whole backpack full of fresh corn that he had just picked that morning. We had a real feast with our friends, the Butlers.

We drove back to Portland, moved into our funky little duplex and Alan started school. I took care of our home and child. Aunt Dede had died the October before and left me a small inheritance. That is pretty much what we lived on. Because money was scarce, we ate a lot of meals at both sets of parent's homes. I would call my Mother-in-law and ask what was for dinner. She would say "GOK", meaning God Only Knows. We usually wound up there for dinner.

Alan was on leave from his job, so was able to attend classes without the worry of having to go to work. Graduation day was a joyous day for us. His brother Jim received his law degree on the same day, so his parents were split between the two commencement ceremonies, but we got together afterwards for a big celebration. It took Alan 14 years to complete his degree with time off to work and save money for tuition and three and a half years in the Army but he was determined to finish.

After graduation, he quit his job at Chevron Asphalt and got a job working for Georgia Pacific Corp. as an inside salesman.

In early 1970, we bought a house in Portland. It was an old home but had a lot of charm and we had great plans to fix it up. It was good to be able to have our families to our home without being crammed in. Also, another baby was on the way, which was another good reason to get the house ready. We planted a garden in the back yard, with all the usual vegetables. About the first of August, we knew we were going to have a bumper crop of tomatoes. Our sweet little Patrick decided one day that he was going to help Mama and Daddy do the harvesting. He picked all of the green tomatoes from the vines and filled his wagon. He pulled it to the back door and informed me that "I helped, Mama." I was dismayed to lose all of those lovely tomatoes, but couldn't get mad at him. He thought he was doing a good thing. I called my Mama to beg for help and she suggested that I make green tomato relish. So, I canned green tomato relish and we ate it for quite a while on everything I could think of.

Alan was informed in September 1970, that he was being transferred to Great Falls, Montana as an outside salesman. He left in October, before the baby was born. So, Patrick and I moved in with Mama and John and waited for the birth. The house was put up for sale and sold quickly. The sale was not to be final until we moved.

Alan was able to make a trip home towards the end of October, but only for a weekend. The baby was due the middle of November and I was very afraid that I would have it without my husband there, but he was home on the 13th of November for the weekend. Steven LeRoy Perkins was born on the 14th of November and his Daddy was able to spend the next week at home with us. He came home again at Christmas but had to return within a couple of days. The boys and I left Portland on the 31st of December and flew to Great Falls,

Montana. I was apprehensive about the trip, having to take care of a 2-year-old and a 1-month-old child.

The airport in Great Falls was built on a bluff and to get into town, we had to drive down the hill and take the bridge across the Missouri River. Much to my amazement, the river was frozen over. I had never seen a river that was frozen before. If an ice cube hits the Willamette River in Portland, the whole town freaks. In Great Falls that day, it was 21 degrees below zero.

We stayed in a motel until the moving van came with our stuff. Besides a frozen leather sofa bed and 14 jars of frozen canned peaches that I worked very hard to put up, our belongings arrived safely. The moving company moved us in on a Tuesday and Alan left on Wednesday to go to Canada to work. His sales route was from Great Falls to Edmonton, Alberta. In the short time he was home, he taught me to drive on the icy roads and where the grocery store was. Other than that, I was pretty much on my own until he came home on Friday evening.

After a year in the rental house, it looked like we were going to stay in Great Falls, so we started looking for a house to buy. We found a nice large house with three bedrooms and a finished basement. We moved in and had a good time fixing it up to make it our home. Even though Alan was traveling from Monday to Friday, I had a good time in that house. Patrick started kindergarten in Great Falls and loved it. He already knew how to read and was a "student" from the start. In 1972, I found out I was pregnant again with the baby due in February. I was lonesome most of the time and tired. I had a 5-year-old and a very busy 2-year-old to take care of by myself.

After a month of labor and a visit to the hospital the week before, Jeffrey John Perkins was born on February 24, 1973, 3 days before his Daddy's birthday. We knew we did not want any more children, so I had my tubes tied right after delivery. In the meantime, Alan found out he was moving again. He was being transferred to Billings, Mt. for training as a manager. He told me about the move while I was still in the hospital. He had to leave the day after he took me home. By God's good grace. Alan's cousin Bill and his family were moving from Ohio to Spokane, WA and came thru Great Falls. They stopped to see us and stayed a week to take care of the boys and me. They were sent from Heaven, I am sure. With a child I had to get to school every day in very cold weather a 2-year-old to watch like a hawk and a newborn to take care of along with being sore from surgery, I was in rough shape. Bill and Sandy took care of the older boys, cleaned my house, cooked the meals and Bill even went to the base commissary and stocked up on food. When Alan came home on Friday night, all was well with our world.

We put the house up for sale and started thinking about moving again. The house did not sell until September. We moved in October. Billings did not offer Kindergarten in their public schools, but I found a private school for Patrick. We knew this move would be temporary, but we did not know where we would go after his training was complete. Life has a way of testing us. 6 months after we arrived in Billings, Georgia Pacific moved us back to Great Falls and six months after that, they moved us to Calgary, Alberta Canada, and six months after that, they moved us to Tacoma, WA. Poor Patrick had gone to 6 different schools by the time he had finished the first grade. Georgia Pacific could not guarantee that we would not have to move again soon. When I heard that, I said no more. I could not move again, and I would not do that to Patrick. The poor little guy had no friends and was afraid to make any for fear that he would have to leave them again. We agreed that Alan would leave Georgia Pacific. He went to work for State Farm Insurance Company as an agent. We bought a house in the North End of Tacoma and settled in. My dream was to spend two Christmases in the same house. We spent 7 in that house, but as the boys grew, we knew we were going to outgrow it. Also, I had started to work for Alan on a part-time basis. The office was 14 miles from home, and we were driving two cars, so we started looking for a home closer to the office. After several months, we found a place in Parkland, WA just a mile from the office. It was a large house with 5 bedrooms, an upstairs and a basement on 2 acres of land. A barn, a chicken coop and several other outbuildings were also on the property. We bought the house, settled in, and became gentlemen farmers. We stayed in that house for 34 years.

While working for State Farm, Alan was able to earn some very nice trips. We went to Monaco, Bermuda, Hawaii twice, Acapulco and Orlando, Florida. Patrick went with us to Acapulco and Jeff went with us to Orlando. The trip to Acapulco was fun for Pat. He was a big hit with some of the wives of other agents. We went to one dinner way up in the hills overlooking the city. Five or six of us crammed into a taxi and held on for dear life as we careened around bends and up hills to the restaurant. Patrick was sitting away from us at the table and the ladies were feeding him drinks on the sly. He was feeling no pain when we returned to the hotel.

We have always had music in our lives. I play the piano and sang in my school and church choirs. Alan played the drums in his high school band. Patrick played the trombone, Steven played the drums and Jeffrey played the trumpet for a while. All of us now have our favorites to listen to and we respect the others right to listen to what they prefer.

We have been married for almost 55 years, some good and some not so good, but always challenging and always fun. We still love each other dearly. We have 7 beautiful grandchildren who are the lights of our lives.

Life continues as it should.

CHAPTER 26

Life with a Traveling Salesman

Alan Perkins

In 1970, we moved to Montana. Alan worked for Georgia Pacific Corporation as an outdoor salesman. His sales route was from Great Falls to Edmonton Alberta and some other areas in Alberta and Northwest Montana.

We moved into our house on a Tuesday, and he left for work on Wednesday and returned home Friday evening. I had a very quick introduction to Great Falls and driving on thick ice. I had a 2-year-old and a 1-month-old and was scared to death. What would I do about buying groceries, getting warm clothes for myself finding a doctor for the boys and for me. I had never experienced below zero weather before, let alone lived in it. I took the big step, bundled up the boys and myself and ventured out. I found a store where I could buy a warm hat, scarf and gloves for myself and a good pair of boots so my feet would not freeze. I made sure the boys were well clothed for the cold weather. I found the grocery store and stocked up on food that was easy to fix and that Patrick would eat.

God was certainly looking out for us because we moved into a house right across the street from the town's leading pediatrician. Oh, how thankful I was. I quickly made appointments for the boys and found out where the clinic was.

I settled into life with just the boys during the week and Alan home on the weekend. It was a bit of a shock to me when he needed his clothes washed and ironed and ready for him to leave on Monday morning. He liked to stay home with the boys on the weekend and all I wanted to do is go out and have some adult conversation. This was an ongoing concern for me all the time he had that job.

When we bought our home, I thought my feelings would change. We started going to church and I joined a women's business sorority. I finally had some other women to talk to. Unfortunately, my plans did not work out. The women in the group were pretty much of a click unto themselves and were not happy about including a newcomer to the group. They were not interested in the news of the day or what was going on in the world. They only wanted to talk about nursing babies, what was the best disposable diaper and what was the newest movie they saw. I was disappointed.

I got depressed one evening and packed suitcases for the boys and me and was ready to drive to Portland and be with my parents. Before I put the bags in the car, I knew that I could not take the boys away from their Daddy and I did not want to leave him either. I just wanted some adult company for a change. I decided that this was my life for the time being and I needed to change my perspective on things.

It did improve when we moved to Billings. Alan was in training to become a manager and was home in the evenings. He did not travel for his job from then on.

And life continues.

CHAPTER 27

The Joys Of Moving

Just before Alan and I were married, we rented a duplex in Vancouver, WA. It was a funny little place with a purple door and purple walls inside. Alan found out about 3 weeks before the wedding that he was being transferred to El Segundo, CA. so we informed the purple lady that we would not be renting the place. Alan left for California two weeks before the wedding, worked a week, found us a place to live and came home a week before the wedding. After a three-day honeymoon to Southern Oregon and the Oregon Coast, we returned to Portland, watched the moving company pack, and load all our stuff, packed the Corvair convertible and headed South. We decided to make the trip South an extended honeymoon and drove down the coast to LA County. Move #1.

When we found out a baby was on the way, we knew that we needed a place that was less expensive than the one we had, so we moved to Harbor City, CA to a large apartment complex. That was move #2.

Patrick was about 6 months old when I decided to go back to work, and we moved to Hawthorne to be near the babysitter and be nearer Alan's work and my work. Move #3.

Alan took some classes at UCLA, working towards getting his bachelor's degree. Then he found out that he was in danger of losing some of his credits and that he had to finish his degree on campus at Portland State. The Los Angeles area was in turmoil with the Manson murders and riots all over the area. Home burglaries were up considerably, and we were not comfortable raising a family in that environment, so we decided to move back to Portland, mainly so that he could finish school. John flew down to help us drive the car and a U-Haul towing the other car back to Portland. Mama found a little duplex for us to live in. It cost us all of $50.00 a month. Move #4.

We moved in and Alan went to school full time. He took a leave of absence from work so that he could concentrate on school. He finished all his classes that first semester back, quit his job in California and found a job with Georgia Pacific Corporation. We bought a house in Southeast Portland. Move #5.

In April 1970, we found out another baby was on the way, so we were doubly glad we bought the house.

In June, after 14 years of school, working, military service, more school and more working, Alan finally received his diploma. We were excited to have a new home of our own and to have another baby on the way. We were really going to settle down. No such luck - - - In September, Alan found out that he was being transferred to Great Falls, Montana as an outside salesman. They wanted him there as soon as possible. So, Patrick and I moved in with Mama and John and we put our house up for sale. I stayed in Portland until after the baby was born in November. Alan managed to come home for a weekend in October, but I had nightmares about having the baby without my husband there. He managed a weekend in November—arriving home on November 12th. Steven LeRoy Perkins was born on November 14th. His Daddy was able to stay with us for a week.

Our house sold, a moving van came and packed all our stuff and the boys, and I flew to Great Falls on December 31st. Alan had found a house for us to rent and on January 5th our belongings arrived and were unloaded. Move # 6.

Great Falls was 20 degrees below zero when we arrived. I did not know that rivers froze over, and I had no idea how to drive on the icy roads. Alan had to give me a crash course on how to drive and where the grocery store and the pharmacy were. Our belongings arrived on a Tuesday and Alan left on Wednesday for Canada and his sales route. I quickly learned where the grocery and drug store were and the local doctor's office. Life went on with Alan traveling from

LIFE AND LOVE CONTINUE

Monday to Friday and me staying home taking care of our 2 precious boys. After about a year in the rental house, we decided to take the plunge and look for a house to buy. We did not like renting. We felt pretty sure that we were not going to be transferred anymore. We found a lovely home, made an offer and it was accepted. We packed up our things and moved into our own home. Move # 7.

Again, we found out another baby was due in February. On February 24, Jeffrey John Perkins was born. Patrick had started kindergarten and loved going to school. We were getting used to the routine. While I was still in the hospital, Alan was told that he was being transferred to Billings, Montana for management training. We did not know where we would go after Billings. We put our house on the market and I stayed in Great Falls trying to sell the house while Alan traveled back and forth on the weekends. Finally, the house sold, and we moved to Billings in October. Billings did not have public kindergarten, so I found a private school to for Patrick. Move # 8.

After a year of training, we were transferred back to Great Falls. So, the moving van came to pack up our things and we drove both cars back to Great Falls. We were lucky and bought our same house back. Move #9.

We were in Great Falls for seven months when a transfer was made to Calgary Alberta, Canada. Alan was to train a Canadian to do the management job. Move #10.

We knew that we only had a year's visa to work in Canada, so that was not a surprise when we were transferred to Tacoma, WA. Move #11. We were happy that we would be closer to family in Portland and that the boys would be able to have a closer relationship with them, but with this last move, Patrick will have gone to 6 different schools before he finished the first grade, and I was tired of not being settled in one place. I wanted a forever home and wanted to spend 2 Christmas holidays in the same house. I told Alan that I could not move anymore, and he agreed with me. Georgia Pacific could not guarantee that we would stay in Tacoma, so he decided to quit. We were in the process of buying a house and while the State Farm agent was doing the paperwork to insure the home, he was talking to Alan about the opportunities at State Farm. Alan was interested and interviewed with the area manager. He was offered a job as an agent and accepted the position. He had quite a bit of training to do before he could go to work and had to pass the test to get his State of Washington Insurance license. In the Fall, he quit his job at Georgia Pacific and went to work for State Farm. The hours were long, and the pay wasn't great to begin with, but at least he was home every night. That was a real plus.

With change, Life Continues.

CHAPTER 28

The House on North 29th

We had traveled to Tacoma to look for a house to buy but had no luck finding a place. A realtor was helping us look and when we drove back to Calgary, he called to let us know that he had just listed the perfect house for us.

Alan packed up the car and drove back to Tacoma to sign the papers. The poor realtor was nervous until I got there to sign also. The house was everything I wanted and more.

After flying back to Calgary, the movers packed up and we said goodbye to Canada and drove to our new home in Tacoma. Because we were coming from out of the United States, we were subject to inspection by the U.S. Customs. The moving truck was sealed in Calgary and would have to be released in Tacoma. The truck arrived at our house but had to wait about 2 hours for the Customs agents to arrive. They were not happy movers.

A big reason for buying the house was a tree house in the back yard. He knew that the boys would love it. It was also a draw for the neighborhood kids and our boys were able to make friends quickly.

When we moved into the house in the North End of Tacoma, we were certain that we would not have to moved again unless we chose to. I had a goal of spending two Christmases in one house. So, we settled into a routine with Alan working, the boys going to school and participating in some extracurricular activities. We joined the local Methodist church, and the boys went to Sunday School and joined us in the church service. They were all three baptized in the church. Patrick sang in the youth choir, singing a solo during one

Christmas season, was a candle lighter and when he was a little older, read the scripture during the church service. I taught the Sunday School class for the preschoolers and Alan was able to attend some very interesting and educational adult Sunday School classes.

Alan and I joined the young adult group called Serendipity. We attended social activities for the adults while the children were well supervised. One of our favorite activities was a Progressive Dinner with each course at a different home. It gave us a great opportunity to interact with other couples about our same age and eat some great food.

Another fun activity was a Watch Night party on New Year's Eve. One of the members had a birthday on January 1st and we presented her with a beautiful cake. When she cut into it, she could not cut clear through the cake. The host had taken a piece of foam rubber to the bakery and had it beautifully ice and decorated. We all laughed until our sides hurt. The look on her face was priceless.

After Alan and I moved to our house in Parkland, we hosted a Hawaiian Luau. One of the couples had family from Hawaii and they gave Hula lessons. We roasted a whole pig. We had an above ground spit that some of the men turned all night. That was some of the best pork I had ever had.

In 1977, we heard about an exchange student program with High School students from Japan. We were interviewed and accepted as a host family. In July, we met Miyuki, our student from Kitakushu, Japan. She was here on a one-year visa to attend high school in the Tacoma area.

Within a couple of weeks of her arriving, we took her on a trip to Montana, and Alberta, Canada. She was able to see some of the old west from the Lewis and Clark expedition to the Oregon Trail.

Miyuki was a good cook and fixed us some great meals. One of my favorites was sukiyaki. It was fascinating watching her cook with the chopsticks.

Miyuki had the opportunity to meet the Mayor of Tacoma. She was nervous and kept her hands and arms around her stomach. I asked her if she had "butterflies" in her stomach. She was totally stumped

LIFE AND LOVE CONTINUE

by that statement. I explained it was an expression to indicate that someone was very nervous. She laughed and relaxed after that.

It was a challenge having a teenage girl in our home with three small boys. If we were to have an exchange student again, I would certainly wait until our children were older and were able to appreciate the experience a little better. Miyuki did not go home to Japan after her year with us. She moved to California and continued her education there. After a couple of letters, we lost track of her.

The city of Tacoma put on a great Fourth of July fireworks show on Commencement Bay. We lived close to a good viewing area and would sit on the porch and yard of the neighbors across the alley from us. During the Bi-Centennial celebration, we had company from out of town and had a barbecue in our back yard and watched the fireworks from our neighbor's yard. Our visitors said that they couldn't have picked a better way to spend the holiday. It was a great family time for everyone.

Soon after Alan started working for State Farm Insurance, he was asked to join the Kiwanis Club. He became President of the club and is one of the Parkland-Spanaway Kiwanis Club's oldest members.

One of the first district conventions we went to was in the Tri-Cities—Pasco, Richland and Kennewick, WA. The Tri-Cities are in Southeastern Washington and in the summer, are very hot. The convention was in August. We decided to make a family vacation out of the trip and packed up our tent trailer with all of our gear and off we went to Eastern Washington. The city of Pasco has a lovely park along the Columbia River and there is a nice area for camping. Our tent trailer had no air conditioning, but we figured we would be okay in the evening and we were not going to spend a lot of time there during the day. Well, our plans quickly went haywire when the park rangers told us that the whole septic system had broken down and there was no water, showers, or toilet facilities available. They hurriedly put some portable toilets up, but we had to rely on the water that was in our trailer tanks for both washing, and drinking. And, the temperature shot up to 110 degrees during the day. The rangers parked us in the swampy area of the park and the mosquitos were terrible. We were smashing them all night long on the canvas ceiling of the trailer.

McDonald's was our restaurant of choice as we had limited funds available for eating and it was too hot to cook in the trailer and with no water available, it was difficult to cook a meal. Anyway, McDonald's was air conditioned. On Saturday evening, we had not signed up for a convention event, so we decided to splurge and take the boys to a movie. As we were driving down the main road of Pasco, I saw a movie theater that said Air Conditioned! The movie was "Raiders of the Lost Ark." My first thought was that it would be a good wholesome movie for the boys to watch—all about finding Noah's ark, and it would be cool inside. Was I ever wrong! It was freezing inside. We were dressed in shorts and tank tops. I thought the boys were overly excited about a historical, religious movie, but maybe it was the air conditioning that hyped them up. The opening credits were running, then the next thing I saw was a basket full of snakes. I buried my head on Alan's shoulder and went to sleep.

I participated in a couple of the ladies' events at the convention (women could not be members of Kiwanis at that time). I enjoyed myself, but was embarrassed because I had not been able to shower or wash my hair and I had wrinkled clothes. I won a prize at one of the luncheons and had to walk up on stage to receive it, much to my embarrassment.

The convention in the Tri-Cities was the first of many district and international conventions that I have attended. Women were allowed to join Kiwanis in 1987 and soon after, I joined. I eventually became president of my club and then went on to become Lieutenant Governor of our local division. I had so much fun, learned a lot about leadership and made some lifelong friends along the way. I was able to attend several International Conventions over the years and broadened the friendships by doing so. But, I will always remember that first Kiwanis Convention I attended. I can laugh at the experience now, but I sure wasn't laughing then.

Family get-togethers and dinners have always been important events in our household. When we were in the house in the North End, we had Thanksgiving dinners with the Perkins grandparents

LIFE AND LOVE CONTINUE

and Christmas dinners with the Talbott grandparents. Our family has had some beautiful dinners at the table Mama purchased so many years ago.

Life does continue even with a lot of twists and turns.

CHAPTER 29

The Red House

The Red House

In 1981 when we bought the big house in Parkland, it was a dirty cream color. I knew that I wanted a barn red house, but it took a couple of years for me to get it. It had been a long time since it had been painted. Alan scraped and primed the entire house. Instead of buying primer paint, he mixed all the extra paint that we had, used it as primer and for a while, the house was a pink polka dot house. Finally, we could afford to have it painted a barn red with off white trim.

The color shook up the neighbors. They did not like it, but they got used to it and admitted that it looked better than it did. From the time we first painted, it was called the "Red House".

LIFE AND LOVE CONTINUE

The yard had fruit trees, lots of berry plants, grapes, and a large space for a garden. We planted all the usual vegetables, peas, beans, corn, tomatoes, lettuce, and carrots. We also tried to grow broccoli, cauliflower, artichokes, zucchini, pumpkins, turnips, onions, and garlic. It was fun canning and freezing all our bounty.

The fruit trees produced plums, pears, apples, and cherries. The house had a cold room in the basement for storage of canned goods. I had a goal one summer of filling all the shelves with home canned fruit and jams and jellies and I did. I canned peaches, pears, plums, applesauce, apricots and even made my own fruit cocktail. I made strawberry, raspberry, blackberry, loganberry, blackcap, and blueberry jams. The shelves were full. I gained a lot of confidence in my ability to provide for my family and it brought back sweet memories of my Nanama.

With the amount of land we had, we were finally able to have dogs. Steven was in a 4H group that showed dogs at the fair. He showed two of his dogs at both the Pierce County fair and the Puyallup Fair. Snoopy was a special dog. She was a faithful friend to all of us.

There was a chicken house behind the barn. With some elbow grease and modifications, we let some chickens move in. We had both hens and roosters, so were never sure about the eggs that we gathered. Sometimes there were baby chicks in them. Some of the chickens were good layers but did not want to give up the eggs easily. They pecked at the hands that got too close.

When Jeff was in the fifth grade, his class tried to hatch and raise some baby chicks. They had the eggs in an incubator in their classroom. During Spring Break, the student teacher took the incubator with the eggs home with her. She was not sure how to operate the incubator and turned it up to high. She fried all but one of the eggs. The egg hatched and the class named the chick Huey. Jeff was the only student who returned a permission slip to take home one of the chicks. So, Jeff brought Huey home. Poor Huey. He had some major problems. He was so large that he could not sit on the perch. He rolled off. His morning wakeup call was not normal and sounded like he was in an echo chamber. Poor thing, he did not know what to do with a lady chicken. He was totally lacking in chicken social skills. Jeff's classmates would come to visit Huey, but only laughed at him. Finally, the other chickens got tired of him and pecked him to death. He was buried in the back part of the garden.

We raised a variety of other animals. We had geese, a goat, some sheep and two pigs. We also had a flock of turkeys. One of the turkey's dressed out at 36 pounds. Turkeys that you buy in the store are all tucked in and easy to get into a pan and fit into the oven. This one was not. I had to tie the legs together, pull them up and over the top to tie to the other roaster handle. It barely fit into my oven. It sure did look funny, but boy did it taste good. Because he was so big, I frantically called friends and begged them to come to dinner. I made all of the standard side dishes to a turkey dinner and we did have a feast.

Several times we had meals consisting of only what we grew in the garden. It felt very good to be able to look at the table and see the results of all the hard work we put into providing food for our family.

We continued to raise a variety of fruits and vegetables and continued to use the freezers, but after raising two pigs, our animal raising days were over. Only cats and dogs were allowed now.

Alan became involved in homemade winemaking and converted part of the fruit room into a wine cellar. He joined the "Puget Sound Amateur Wine and Beer Making Club." He learned a lot about the art of winemaking and improved his skills considerably. He even won some ribbons at the fair.

Raising three boys was a true joy, but also a big job with a lot of work involved. They had chores to do and most of the time, pretty good about getting them done. When it was Jeffrey's turn to feed the chickens and geese, he hated it. The geese were mean and would flap their wings at him, hitting his legs and leaving bruises. Fortunately, the red house and the property around it allowed them to grow and mature into the outstanding men they are today.

They all had diverse interests while growing up. Patrick was the studious one, being more academically inclined. He went directly from high school to college earning a degree in Journalism. He played trombone in the high school band for 3 years and worked

LIFE AND LOVE CONTINUE

part-time at Burger King. Steven was the athlete in the family. He played football for the Franklin Pierce Cardinals. Unfortunately, he was hurt several times and his football days were cut short. He had a couple of jobs during his high school years, one working at Ernst Hardware and the other working at a Pizza parlor. I think one of Steven's favorite activities was skipping school. He became very good at forging his dad's signature but had a harder time with mine. Steve attended Bates Technical School after graduation, studying robotics.

Jeffrey was keenly interested in the military and joined the Junior ROTC class at Washington High School. He was a member of the drill team for 4 years, during which time the team won several State championships. Jeff had a job his junior and senior years in high school working at a tire shop. His Dad and I signed a deferred enlistment form which enabled him to enlist in the Air Force at 17 years old, but graduate from high school and be 18 years old when he went to basic training. He had several assignments in the States and was in Italy, Korea (twice) and Afghanistan. He spent 20 years in the Air Force and served his country proudly. We are very proud of all three of our boys.

We continued to keep the property up. We added a deck and a hot tub and did a complete remodel of the kitchen. Both of us worked and were fortunate to be able to do some traveling. All three boys married while we lived in the red house and all three boys brought their wives and children there. Two of the boys, Patrick and Jeffrey and their families moved back in for a short time until they found housing in the area.

After Patrick and his family moved into their own home in Tacoma, and we were truly empty nesters, we started thinking about downsizing and getting a smaller place with no steps and no yard to take care of. The large house and all the property were getting too much for us to take care of, but the thought of moving again was overwhelming. We had lived in the house for 34 years and it was full of all our family treasures and so many memories.

After a lot of thinking and looking, we found the ideal community to live in. It is called "Brookdale Greens" and is a 55 and older, gated community of manufactured homes. Our house is about

1500 square feet with a 2-car attached garage. There are two stairs up to the front door and one step into the house from the garage. We moved into the house in October 2015, but it took us another year to sell the red house. It was sad to leave that house, but we are busy making new memories.

With change, life goes on.

CHAPTER 30

Feeding Three Growing Boys
Or
The Dreaded Brown Pan

When you have three growing boys to feed, cooking a meal that everyone will eat and like is a real challenge. One doesn't like onions, one doesn't like carrots, one doesn't like peas and all three don't like Brussel sprouts.

When I introduced a new food to them, I wanted them to at least taste it. If they did not like it, okay, at least they tried it. I remember poor Patrick sitting at the dinner table until 8 pm with a quarter of a small brussel sprout on his plate. I really wanted him to at least try it, but he would not budge. No way, no how would he put that vile thing in his mouth. I finally gave up and concluded that Patrick did not like brussel sprouts.

All three of the boys are grown and have families of their own. I'm sure all the grandkids have heard stories about the dreaded brown pan and the leftovers that were served in it and are very glad that Grandma no longer has it. Even though the thought of that pan does not bring back the fondest memories, we do all have our own memories of sitting around the table staring at that dreaded brown pan.

Life goes on even if we do not like parts of it.

CHAPTER 31

Pat and Jo-Elle

After graduation from High School, Patrick went to the University of Oregon and majored in Journalism. Driving him to Eugene with all his belongings was one of the hardest things I ever had to do. He was the first child to leave home and I knew that he would never be back on a long-term basis again.

He did well in school and seemed to enjoy his classes. He joined a fraternity and moved into the fraternity house. He went to a party and dance one evening and met Jo-Elle, a freshman at the University. She was from LaGrande, Oregon and was studying Anthropology and Geology. We were glad to hear he was dating and attending some of the social activities. It wasn't long until they became a couple. We drove to Eugene one weekend to meet her, and we heartedly approved. We thought her a very nice girl and very good for Patrick.

At some point a promise ring was given and things became a lot more serious. During Pat's senior year, they rented an apartment together. Patrick graduated with a bachelor's degree in journalism and went to work for the Benton Bulletin, a weekly paper in Philomath, Oregon. He was the editor of the paper and wrote some of the articles. Alan and I received a copy of the paper every week and looked forward to reading his editorials.

The next June, Jo-Elle graduated and a month later, they were married in "The Old Church" in Portland. As we gathered the day before for the rehearsal, we found the door to the church locked. We waited outside for a long time, but no one came. Another wedding party showed up for their ceremony that evening and could not get

LIFE AND LOVE CONTINUE

in. We rehearsed outside on the sidewalk and when someone finally opened the building, we had only about 15 minutes to rehearse inside before the other group had to get ready.

Even with the odd rehearsal, the wedding was beautiful, and the kids were off on their honeymoon. We drove back to Tacoma without our oldest son.

They moved into his apartment in Philomath where he finished his one-year obligation to the Bulletin. From there, they moved to LaGrande in Eastern Oregon where Patrick had a job with the La Grande Observer as a sports reporter. It was always exciting for Patrick to be able to apply skills learned to practical purposes.

Our first Grandchild, Emma Dora was born on June 29, 1993. Pat called us right away and his first words were "it's a girl and she has red hair." We made a fast trip to LaGrande to see this wonder child. After having three boys, I was over the moon about having a granddaughter. Two years after Emma was born, along came Susanna Noel. She was our Thanksgiving baby, and we were lucky enough to be there when she was born.

After a lot of hard work and long hours and sacrifice, we were so proud to be in the audience when Jo-Elle received her master's degree from Eastern Oregon University. Now to find a job. Nothing was available in either Oregon or Washington, but she was able to get a teaching job in Blythe, California. Blythe is in Southern California located along Interstate 10 only about three miles from the Arizona border. It is situated along the Colorado River.

Patrick was pretty much at a standstill in his job at the Observer, so they made the decision to move to Blythe. They arrived in there with only Jo-Elle being employed and no real prospects for Patrick. There was no newspaper in Blythe. He was facing a career change, but what to do. His father-in-law suggested that he substitute teach until he decided what he wanted to do. The administration said that they would hire him as a full-time teacher if he would agree to complete the work for his teaching certificate. So, after substituting for a year, he went to work full time at the high school and drove 80 miles one way twice a week to The College of the Desert in Palm Desert to complete the requirements for his teaching certificate. He would teach all day, then get in the car and drive to class, drive home, eat, maybe study, go to bed and get up the next day and teach all day. He received his credentials and was certified to teach public school in the State of California. Both Pat and Jo-Elle worked in the Blythe school district for 11 years, but in 2013, made the decision to leave California and move back to Tacoma. Neither one of them had jobs at the time, but they looked forward to being out of Blythe.

So, in June 2013, Patrick, Jo-Elle, Emma, Susie, Evan (Emma's boyfriend), Sephie the dog and three cats arrived in Tacoma and moved in with us. Finally, all my children were back in Tacoma.

Patrick went to work in the University Place School District teaching High School Juniors Advanced Placement English and Jo-Elle went to work in the Franklin Pierce School District teaching gifted elementary school children. Emma got a job at Francesca's clothing boutique at the Tacoma Mall and Susie went to Washington High School.

The girls are now grown. Susie graduated from Evergreen State College in Olympia and is married to Jeremy and lives in Honolulu, HI. Emma lives in Yucca Valley, California and is the manager of a high-end boutique in Palm Springs. She is married to Logan.

With the marriage of Patrick and Jo-Elle, I had become a mother-in-law. It was going to be a whole new experience for me. While I was growing up, my mother did not have a close relationship with her mother-in-law, nor was I allowed to have a close relationship with my mother-in-law, so I was not sure how I was to react. I only knew that I never wanted to be an interfering mother-in-law or to give unsolicited advice. My son's wives had their own way of living and doing things and I wanted to make sure that I honored that. I have been blessed with daughter- in-laws who are not only lovely, intelligent ladies, excellent mothers, but are sweet and kind to me. I was not blessed with any daughters, but I did get the three of the best daughters-in-law ever.

Even thru life's changes, life and love continue.

CHAPTER 32

The Weddings of Jeffrey and Jennifer

In October 1995, Jeffrey met Jennifer. Three weeks later they were married in a chapel in Las Vegas, NV. Alan and I were not able to get to the wedding. I had just gotten out of the hospital the day before and was unable to travel. I talked to Jennifer on the phone but was not able to meet her or her parents. They planned a formal wedding in January 1996 in a chapel on Edwards Air Force Base in California. We decided to be there for that wedding. We flew into Long Beach airport with Steven, Patrick, Jo-Elle and Emma. We rented a van and drove to Rosamond, just outside the base. There was a very nice hotel that would accommodate all of us. Mama and my niece Debbie were there also.

Jennifer's family had planned a beautiful wedding and reception. Everyone was there waiting for the start of the ceremony. Everyone was there except the Pastor. He was an hour late because he forgot and thought the wedding was the next week. Emma was to be the flower girl, but after waiting so long, she was tired and would not walk down the aisle. The pastor finally got there, and the ceremony proceeded. Jennifer looked beautiful. Her Dad was dressed in his marine uniform. Jeff, his best man Keith and Jeff's friend Steve were all dressed in their dress blues. They all looked pretty good. Steven and Patrick were groomsmen for Jeff. The reception was held in a hall on base. It was so much fun. Jeff and I danced to the song "Wind Beneath my Wings" and I cried.

The newlyweds left on their honeymoon to Tacoma and our house, while Alan and I took Steven, Pat, Jo-Elle and Emma to Disneyland. Pat had not been there since he was a tiny baby and Steven had never been there. Jo-Elle had been there many times. The weather was not very cooperative, and the park issued yellow rain ponchos to everyone. A picture of Mickey was on the back of each poncho. It was a little hard to find a specific person as everyone looked alike. We had one room at the Disneyland hotel for all of us. There were three double beds, one for Pat and Jo-Elle, one for Alan and I and one for Steven and Emma. That was a new experience for Steven, sleeping with a two-year-old. We only had one day in the park and wanted to take advantage of all we could. We went on rides, saw many displays, shopped, and ate and walked and walked. Grandpa and I gave up first and went back to the hotel. Patrick and Emma came along a little later when Emma was about to fall asleep. Steven and Jo-Elle held out until the very end. They were the daring ones and went on all the scary rides that the rest of us would not. We all had such a good time and made some lasting memories, but it was time to pack up and head for the airport and home. We had a wedding reception for Jeff and Jennifer to plan in Tacoma.

In the meantime, Jeff and Jenn were at our house in Tacoma freezing to death. The furnace would not start, and it was 40 degrees in the house when we arrived home. Alan got the furnace going and we warmed up. We had a reception at the house for friends in Tacoma so that they could meet our new daughter-in-law. The kids went back to California and settled into their home on Edwards Air Force Base. They have three children, Michaela, Zander, and Samantha. Michaela is married to Alex. Zander and Samantha are both working and living on their own.

Jeff and Jenn have moved to Mississippi. They have a very nice home there and enjoy the area. Both are working and enjoying their life together. Michaela and Alex have also moved to Mississippi and are expecting a baby in June. Our family is growing and we love it.

Love will make life continue as it should.

CHAPTER 33

Singapore

Steven was the last of our boys to meet his love. He worked for a company that sold and serviced computerized cash registers. He was working with the Nevada Bob's golf shops and his "go to" person was Shareen, the owner's daughter. They started dating and became engaged Christmas of 1998. We were all very pleased and excited. Shareen was a citizen of Singapore and was originally in the United States on a student visa. At the time she met Steven, she had a work visa. The golf shops were sold, and she got a new job. Unfortunately, her new boss did not fill out the proper paperwork for continuation of her work visa and she was subject to deportation. Because of that, Steve and Shareen planned a small wedding in a chapel in Seattle.

Alan and I had driven to Sheppard Air Force Base in Wichita Falls, Texas to visit Jeff and Jenn and their family when Steve called to let us know about the wedding. Because we had missed Jeff's wedding in Las Vegas, we were bound and determined not to miss Steve's wedding. We got in the car the day after we got to Texas and headed home. We made it in time for a very lovely wedding in a beautiful setting in Seattle. Shareen was then able to apply for her green card to stay in the United States. They continued to plan the big wedding for September.

The wedding was beautiful. Shareen wore the dress that my mother made for me and she was beautiful. Her family from Singapore was here to help her celebrate and to get to know the Perkins family. A lovely reception was held at the Tacoma Tennis Club after the ceremony.

After the September wedding, a trip to Singapore was planned to introduce Steve to all of Shareen's extended family. Alan and I were invited to come along. As a side note, Shareen's parents GC and Lucy were lovely people, and we became very fond of them. They were able to spend several months out of the year here in the States visiting not only Shareen, but their other daughter Joyce. They are both gone now and we miss them very much.

Anyway, in January, we flew from Seattle to Japan and then to Singapore. We arrived in Singapore at midnight and were shocked by the heat. One of Shareen's many uncles was there to pick us up in his large van. He introduced himself, then said to just call him "Uncle # 5." There were too many to keep track of names.

We piled into a couple of vans to go to GC and Lucy's home. They lived in a beautiful high rise apartment building.

GC was a gourmet cook but did not cook very much in Singapore. It was too easy to get food from restaurants and markets close to their apartment and it did not heat up the house like cooking a meal would. We had some outstanding food while there.

Singapore has an impressive zoo. They have done an exceptional job of keeping the exhibits as natural as possible. Because they have a good number of nocturnal animals, they have times when the zoo is open to the public at night, G.C. took us to the zoo for the nighttime exhibits. The animals were fascinating, and we were able to see some that we had never seen before. They were all fascinating except the bats! I absolutely hate bats and am scared to death of them. The Singapore bats are very large fruit bats, and their entire exhibit area is inside a netting so that they cannot get loose. The public walks through inside of the netting. If I had not walked through the exhibit, I would have been separated from the rest of the group. So, I walked through with my hands clasped in front of me and my head down. I was teased about the bats for a long time.

It is always fun to visit a new place with someone who lives there. We were able to see things and visit places that the normal tourist does not have a chance to get to or does not know about.

We went to the old Raffles Hotel, made famous before and during WWII. We saw the huge harbor where all the big ships would

LIFE AND LOVE CONTINUE

dock. Downtown Singapore was a shopper's paradise. So many stores to wander through. Singapore has an incredible rapid transit system both below and above ground. We could pretty much go anywhere on the island we wanted to. We had the opportunity to go across the bridge to Malaysia. It was a lot different than Singapore not as clean. Singapore has some to the strictest littering laws of any country in the world. They do not sell chewing gum in the city because they do not want the litter and wrappers all over the ground.

Even with the large population in Singapore, the air is very clean. There is very little smog. Because of their superior rapid transit system and the strict laws the have about purchasing cars, the pollution is controlled. It is very expensive to purchase and own a car and they must be a newer age and pass strict emissions tests.

Many evenings, GC would call down to the restaurant on the street level of their apartment and order dinner for all of us. Lucy and GC had a beautiful round mother-of-pearl inlayed table with a turntable in the center. The food would be put on that turntable, and we would all be able to reach it. GC would tease me and say that everything that he ordered was super spicy hot. He knew that I could not eat the hot food. Usually, only one or two dishes were spicy. When the meal was over and the table cleared, Lucy would bring out a large bowl of cut up papaya and place it in the center of the table. That was dessert and I must say, some of the best dessert I had ever had. Those big bowls of papaya were one of the highlights of the trip.

A large reception was held for Steve and Shareen to introduce Steve to all her Singapore relatives and friends. There were about 200 people there and a nine-course meal was served. We only managed to get 4 courses before we had to get up and follow the bride and groom around to each table to receive their best wishes and a gift. The gifts consisted of red envelopes containing money.

It was very different for Steven and us as his parents, to marry into a family of Chinese descent. It was very reassuring to be so readily accepted by the entire family, all the aunts, uncles and cousins included. Shareen's parents hosted a large family gathering at their home where Steve and Shareen performed the Chinese Tea Ceremony for each couple. The tea ceremony is a tradition honoring the families of the newly married couple. The kids did a marvelous job of honoring their families.

After our time in Singapore, we took a flight to Phuket, Thailand a resort city on an island in the Andaman Sea in the Indian Ocean. The men played golf and the women shopped, swam, had massages and pedicures, and generally had a very relaxing time.

We flew back to Singapore with only a couple of days left before we had to fly home. Both Alan and I felt very honored to be included in this once in a lifetime trip.

Extended family and love help life continue.

CHAPTER 34

Traveling by Motorhome after Retirement

Some years into our married life, Alan and I decided that when we retired, we would buy a motorhome and travel the United States. We have been very fortunate to have been able to travel overseas but have not seen a lot of our own country. Both of us had been to Europe, Alan courtesy of the U.S. Army and me courtesy of the "Cheap Plan."

So, when we retired in 2000, we bought our first motorhome, a Winnebago gas powered rig. Almost immediately, we were hooked. The ability to take our home with us was so much better than staying in motels and eating in restaurants. We joined the Good Sam club and took advantage of the discounts available on lodging in RV Parks. When we plan a trip, we use the big RV book that gives us information on all the Good Sam approved parks in the U.S. and Canada. We are also assured that the parks were clean and well maintained.

It wasn't long before we knew that we would upgrade to a diesel-powered rig, so we bought an Allegro Bus. It had so much more power than the gas rig and easier to go up steep roads. We did not have to shift down and go five to ten miles an hour to go up a hill.

Our first trip was to Blythe, CA to visit Pat, Jo-Elle, and the girls. We parked in their back yard and usually stayed between three weeks to a month in the Winter. Alan wanted to be there in January so he could help set up the Bluegrass Festival. He became hooked on the music. We also made several trips to Florida to visit Alan's brother Jim and we followed Jeff and Jenn from air base to air base around the U.S.

We upgraded our motorhome again to a 2000 Allegro Bus with three slide outs. It has so much more room and we can live comfortably it is for a longer period of time.

We were well on our way to visiting every state in the United States, so we planned a 6-month trip, the end purpose of being in North Carolina with Jeff and Jenn and the grandkids. We started out in September by going to Yellowstone, then we headed up to the high-line and crossed North Dakota and on east. We saw the Mandan Village where Lewis and Clark spent a Winter, saw the Mall of America in Minnesota, the Kiwanis International Headquarters in Indiana and went across into Canada to the Canadian side of Niagara Falls. We were in awe of the power of the water. From Niagara Falls, we headed to Rochester, NY to visit with Alan's cousin Margaret. Rochester is the home of the Kodak Camera Company.

From Rochester, we headed for Fort Ticonderoga in upper New York State. The Fort is located on Lake Champlain and was made famous during the Revolutionary War. From there, our travels took us to Burlington, Vermont and a visit with Alan's cousin Denise and her husband Stanley. From Burlington, we drove South thru Vermont, visiting the area where Alan's mother and her siblings grew up. The LeRoy family farm was in Stamford, VT. It was called the rock farm and you can guess why by looking at the countryside. There are rocks everywhere. The fences are built out of rocks. I am not sure how they plowed the ground in order to plant. They all worked very hard.

We drove across the border into North Adams, Mass. to visit some of the LeRoy family graves, then on to Pittsfield to visit Cousin Shirley.

From Massachusetts, we drove thru Connecticut into New York headed for Long Island and Alan's fraternity brother, Pat Dumas. And we got lost!!! Of all places, Brooklyn, N.Y. Imagine driving around the narrow streets of Brooklyn in a huge 37' motorhome. Because of the tall buildings, we could not determine the direction we were headed. We finally found a street that seemed would take us out of the area and towards our destination of Long Island. The pedestrians were laughing at us. We kept going around the blocks and couldn't find our way out of the area. We both were getting nervous and were not certain if we would have to stop and ask directions. We did not want to get out of the Motorhome if possible.

We finally made our way out of Brooklyn and to Long Island and Pat's home. What a nice man. We enjoyed our visit with him and his wife so much. He took us into the city to see the twin tower site. At the time, it was still a big hole in the ground. The highlight of that part of the trip was a tour of Sagamore Hill, Teddy Roosevelt's home. It is truly an impressive home and reflects his way of living. It was a great family home. We left Pat's house and drove thru New Jersey, Maryland, and Delaware. We went to Virginia and Pennsylvania. While in Pennsylvania, we toured the Gettysburg battlefield and went to Lancaster, in the Amish country. What beautiful, pristine farms they have. The shops were packed with homemade goods.

At several of the places we stopped, we saw a 1960's type, brightly colored V.W. Van with Mom, Dad and three kids living in it. Mom and Dad were homeschooling the kids. Oh, what I would have given to be able to learn history that way.

Washington, DC was on my bucket list. I have always wanted to see it. We crammed as much sightseeing as we could into the short time we had to stay there. My personal challenge was to climb the steps of the Lincoln Memorial without help. And I did it. What a sight. A visit across the Potomac River to Arlington National Cemetery was another highlight. Watching the changing of the guard at the tomb of the Unknown Soldier made me cry. And of course, President Kennedy's grave was impressive, but very sad.

All along the East Coast, we visited Civil War sites: Gettysburg, Bull Run, Richmond, Chancellorsville, Fredericksburg and many more. They all proved to be very interesting and educational. A drive thru Kentucky gave us a view of miles and miles of white fences and blue grass with groups of horses scattered here and there. We stopped in Louisville at the baseball bat factory. It was fascinating to watch them take a chunk of wood and make a customized bat for a specific player. We enjoyed that tour a lot. We drove past Churchill Downs racetrack in Lexington and enjoyed seeing all the horses in the fields that we drove past.

On into Tennessee and to Chattanooga to visit niece Hollis and her family. We drove into North Carolina and to the Biltmore Estate in Ashville. Biltmore is the Vanderbilt estate and is the largest private residence in the U.S. Part of it is off limits to public tours as it is occupied by members of the Vanderbilt family. From Ashville, we drove on to Fayetteville and Jeff and Jenn's house. We parked the motorhome in their yard and enjoyed some down time with our grandkids.

We were able to spend a weekend with nephew Jason and his wife Amber in Lake Wylie, South Carolina and then went to Florida to visit brother Jim in Fort Walton Beach. Going back to Fayetteville for Christmas with the kids proved a great time. We adopted a kitten that Samantha found. I really did not want another pet, but Alan convinced me. Twinkle rode all the way back to Tacoma with us. We did make a stop in Savanah, GA and saw many of the sights of this famous city. We ate dinner at the" Lady and Son's" Restaurant. It is owned by TV chef Paula Dean and her sons. Boy, did they have wonderful cheese biscuits.

We had a great time with Jim on the Gulf Coast of Florida. One of my favorite places to go is Joe Patti's seafood market in Pensacola. It is a marvelous seafood market with a large variety of fish. It is right on the water and the daily catch is off loaded right into the store and the display cases.

After Christmas in North Carolina with Jeff and family, we decided it was time to start heading for home. So, with our kitten Twinkle in tow, and a tearful goodbye, we headed West. We drove the Midwest States and finally reached home about the first of April. We had been gone 6 ½ months. When this trip was over, we could say that we had been in every state in the United States. What good times we had and what great memories we made.

When we first started traveling around the U.S., Alan bought a Golden Age Pass that allowed us to get into the National Parks for free. It is a lifetime pass and gives us the incentive to visit our National Parks. We bought a National Parks Passport and every time

LIFE AND LOVE CONTINUE

we visit a park, we get a stamp in our passport. The passport is good in all National Parks and at all National Monuments. Each visitor center has a dated stamp naming the park or monument. We have seen some incredible sights and learned a lot about the history of our country.

As we see, life continues.

CHAPTER 35

Nine Year Trips

Alan and I have seven wonderful grandchildren. Emma, Pat, and Jo-Elle's oldest daughter is our oldest grandchild.

It had been our wish to take each of the grandchildren on a trip in the Motorhome. We felt that around 9 years old was a good age.

In June 2002, Alan and I were going to a Kiwanis Convention in New Orleans. We offered to take Emma with us. The trip would be an extended visit to Wichita Falls, Texas to see Jeff, Jenn, and their little ones. We would celebrate Emma's ninth Birthday there.

Kiwanis is very good at having activities for the children while the parents are in meetings. We knew that Emma would be in good hands until we were finished with our meetings. After the Kiwanis day was over, we toured around New Orleans. We had so much fun watching her. Uncle Jim even came from Florida to visit for a couple of days.

After the convention was over, we headed for Sheppard, AFB, in Texas and Jeff's house. We had three more grandchildren there and we spent Emma's birthday with them. After a few days there, we headed North, stopping in Oklahoma City to see the sight of the Murrah building bombing. The building had been severely damaged by a bomb and had been turned into a memorial to those who had died.

From Oklahoma City, we drove North to DeSmit, South Dakota and one of the homes of Laura Ingalls Wilder of "Little House on the Prairie" fame. There is quite a good museum there and an outdoor display of life the way it was during the pioneer times. Again, we had such fun watching Emma. She went into little cabins and stores and was able to drive a pony cart around a track.

A stop in Mitchell, S.D. gave us a chance to see the Corn Palace. The outside of the building is entirely covered in corn cobs. It is fascinating, but the real highlight for Emma and me was a doll museum.

Mount Rushmore was our next stop. Oh, My Goodness!!! All I can say about it is "Awesome". The sight of those four heads carved out of the enormous rock is amazing. We stopped at the carving of Crazy Horse also. It is a work in progress and is equally amazing. It will be several years before it is finished. We drove through the Badlands and then into Wyoming and the Devil's Tower Monument. Devil's Tower is a huge monolith in the desert with nothing else around it. It was a stopping point for pioneers coming West. A lot of names were carved on the tower.

From Devil's Tower, we headed to LaGrande and Emma's home. I'm sure she had a good time and saw a lot of the country she had not seen before. I know that we had a great time making memories with her.

Because of the success of Emma's trip, we decided that age nine was a good age for the grandkids to travel with us. They could go only if they wanted to. We were in no way forcing them. It became a much-anticipated trip for them. We let them choose, within reason, where they wanted to go and what they wanted to see.

Susie was interested in dinosaurs and wanted to see dinosaur bones, so we took her to Drumheller, Alberta Canada. There is a big archeological dig there and she would be able to see how they dig up the bones. They also have an extensive museum. Susie was able to go out to the dig site and look for fossils with a group of other young people.

She came back to Tacoma with us and stayed until the family reunion the end of July. We hosted the reunion that year, but we were in the middle of remodeling the kitchen and only had a BBQ and a microwave available outside on the deck. The refrigerator was in the garage. Everyone was very accommodating and had a great time. Again, it was fun making memories with another one of our grandchildren.

Michaela was our next sweet nine-year-old. She was with Pat and Jo-Elle in Los Angeles, and we picked her up at the LA airport. We drove up the California coast, with the first stop being the Channel Islands National Park, then on to the Hearst Castle in San Simeon, then Big Sur, Carmel, and Monterey. Monterey has a first-class aquarium, and it was super fun. We could walk underneath the sharks and, in some areas, felt like we were under the water. From there we drove through San Francisco and across the Golden Gate Bridge then up to the Redwood National Forest on the Northern California Coast. The obligatory tour of the gift shop was taken, along with a walk through those huge trees. From there we drove into Oregon and up the coast, stopping at a myrtle wood factory in Coos Bay, at the Sea Lion Caves and at a lot of the beautiful beaches along the coast. Newport and Lincoln City were the big city stops. We had to make a stop at Moe's chowder house in Lincoln City before we headed for Tillamook and the Blue Heron and Tillamook cheese factories. On up to Cannon Beach and some reminiscing and then into Seaside.

Seaside has a saltwater taffy store. They have tubes coming from the ceiling filled with every flavor of saltwater taffy imaginable. We gave Mikki a paper bag and told her to have at it. She could fill the paper bag with any flavors she wanted. Alan and I wandered around, picked out some flavors we wanted to try and the next time we saw Mikki, her bag was overflowing, and her eyes were as big as saucers. She was the ultimate "kid in a candy store". We did not realize that we had given her the large bag to fill. We had to be very careful and regulate her intake of candy for the rest of the trip.

We drove on up the coast to Astoria with a stop at the site where Lewis and Clark camped for a winter. Then we drove across the bridge over the Columbia River into Washington, then home to Tacoma. What an absolute delight Michaela was to travel with. She was curious, helpful, and never complained.

Zander is our oldest Grandson. We took him from Las Vegas to Tacoma. His Dad was retiring from the Air Force and moving back

LIFE AND LOVE CONTINUE

to Tacoma, so we took Zander up ahead of time and made a nine-year trip out of it. It is always so much fun having the kids along. The simplest object, sight or tourist attraction along the way becomes so much more interesting when seen through their eyes.

Our sweet Samantha chose not to go on a trip with us. We are hoping that someday, she will want to. She is welcome anytime.

We had to wait several years before our Christopher was 9. His trip was to Ouray, Colorado to visit Uncle Jim, Jason, and Amber. Ouray is a small town in Southwestern Colorado and is about 7800 ft. high. It is called the Switzerland of America and is a beautiful place to visit.

As we traveled to Ouray, we drove across Washington, the Northeast corner of Oregon, the Southwest corner of Idaho and Utah, then into Colorado. We stopped at several tourist sites along the way, but the most impressive was Arches National Park in Utah and the Black Canyon of the Gunnison National Park in Colorado.

Jason and Amber and Jim own an R.V. Park in Ouray. One day, shortly after we got there, we were having lunch in the motorhome and Christopher opened the ketchup bottle. It exploded all over him and the table. The look on his face was priceless. We forgot that the high altitude caused the pressure to build up in the container and a possible explosion when the pressure was released.

Christopher was able to go four wheeling in the mountains, tour a gold mine and do some trout fishing. Not quite like fishing in the Ocean, but fun anyway. He had a school friend whose family had moved to Denver, so we drove him across the state to visit his friend for a weekend. He had a good visit with his friend and Grandpa, and I had a quiet weekend. Christopher is great to travel with and we made some great memories with him.

MaryAlice is our youngest grandchild and the last one to take a nine-year trip with us. She wanted to see the Redwood National Forest in Northern California, so we headed down the Oregon Coast. We stopped at the saltwater taffy store again, but this time, remembered to give her a smaller bag to fill up.

There are so many sights to see along the coast. We hit quite a few of them—Haystack Rock in Cannon Beach, the Tillamook and Blue Heron Cheese factories in Tillamook, the Air Museum in Tillamook, Lincoln City and the Aquarium at Newport, the myrtle wood stores, the sea lion caves and into California to the Redwoods. MaryAlice and Grandpa walked the trail through the tall trees. She and I visited the gift shop and took pictures in front of Paul Bunyan and Babe, the blue ox. I have been to the Redwood National Park several times, but love seeing it through the eyes of my grandchildren.

We traveled North to Jacksonville, Oregon to experience the Vortex House. It is the earliest documented mystery spot or gravitational hill in the United States. All kinds of weird things happen—including balls rolling uphill. MaryAlice was astounded at the strange happenings. It defies all logic.

From Jacksonville we drove to Crater Lake. It is one of the premier tourist spots in Oregon and its only National Park. It was a lot of fun to show her such a beautiful spot. On to Bend, Oregon then up to Timberline Lodge on Mount Hood. Tacoma was our next stop. All the grandchildren make great travel companions. They are curious, very helpful, kind, and polite and we couldn't ask for more. The trips we took with them were the highlights of our retirement years. We look back on them with the best of memories.

With Joy, life continues.

CHAPTER 36

Short Trips

Washington

In early 2019, I read an article in the paper about ten small cities that all Washingtonians should visit. As I read the article and read the list of towns, I realized that we had traveled all over the US, been to every state seen some of Europe, Mexico, Canada, and Asia and not really seen our own state. So, using the list as a guide, we planned a summer trip around the State of Washington and included all of those ten cities in our itinerary. Heading South down Interstate 5 to Vancouver, we headed East to Camas and the Pendleton Woolen Mills outlet store. Pendleton products are still expensive, even in the outlet store, but of the highest quality. We drove along the Columbia River to Maryhill Museum and the Stonehenge Memorial, then North on Highway 97 to Goldendale. From Goldendale, on to Toppenish, Sunnyside, Grandview, and Prosser—all wine country towns. They grow a lot of grapes, but also a lot of wheat and other farm produce. After wine country, we headed for Richland and the Hanford B Reactor Site. It was a very interesting tour of the deactivated reactor.

From the Tri-Cities we took highway 124 to Waitsburg, then on to Dayton, Washington. My Grandmother was born in Dayton and several of my relatives are buried there. We were able to find some of the graves and took some pictures of them. On to Colfax, WA. Some more of my relatives are buried there. Both Dayton and Colfax were on the little city list. Up the highway a way, we saw a sign for Riperia, WA. That was the town where the Stuart Family had their hotel. We followed the sign, but got lost and ended up on a dead end road in a wheat field and could not turn around. We had to unhook the car, move it out of the way and turn the motorhome around. Then hook the car up again to get out of there. Fortunately, there was a man their loading hay bales into the back of his truck and he came to our rescue. He knew Riperia well, had even lived there for a time before it was flooded. He gave us good directions to get there and even followed us and gave us a short tour of what was left of the area. The bridge abutments were still there and some of the concrete slabs where buildings were, but no sign of the hotel. It was flooded when the Snake River was dammed up. After visiting with the rancher for a bit and thanking him profusely for his help, we traveled on up Highway 195. The motorhome died on us along the road to Spokane. We had to have it towed into Spokane for repair. Alan's cousin Bill lived in Spokane so we called and begged a place to stay while the motorhome was being fixed. As happened many times in our married life, Bill and Sandy were there when we needed them. After four days, we were able to pick up the motorhome and continue with our trip.

Our next stop was Kettle Falls in the Northeast corner of Washington along the Columbia River. It was an important fishing site for the Native Americans. They have an outstanding museum in the town. We had the privilege of having a personal tour from a gentleman who used to be a teacher at the high school and whose students contributed many items to the museum. The tour of the museum was a highlight of the whole trip.

From Kettle Falls, we drove to Republic and then on to Grand Coulee Dam to watch the light show on the spill way. It was beautiful and unique. From Coulee, we drove to Winthrop. Winthrop is a western themed town with board walks and old country stores. It is a fun place to visit. Unfortunately, I got sick and had to go to the hospital in Omak. They wanted to keep me overnight, but I refused. I said that I would call my doctor when we got home and see him as soon as possible. We were heading home the next day. I was sure that my bleeding ulcer was acting up again. We drove thru the North Cascades National Park on our way to Tacoma. We made it home the next day, I saw the doctor and was okay. We did learn a lot about the different areas of our State and enjoyed the tour very much.

Oregon

After the success of our Washington trip, the next Summer we decided to do the same type of trip in Oregon. We did not have a list of small towns, but I mapped out a route that would take us thru many of the smaller towns throughout Oregon.

We started at Clackamette Park where the Clackamas River and the Willamette River meet in Oregon City. Oregon City is also the end of the Oregon Trail and has a lot of history. The John McLoughlin house is in Oregon City. He was a businessman and mill owner. He was named the "Father of Oregon" because of the help he gave to the American settlers.

From Oregon City, we went South on highway 99 east, sometimes passing over Interstate 5 to Highway 99 West. I was excited to visit Monmouth Oregon and to see the college there. My parents went to school there in the 1930's. From Monmouth, it was South to Philomoth, then East to Lebanon and Sweet Home, then over the freeway again to Junction City. That is the town my parents were headed for on the day they were married.

We avoided the Oregon Coast as much as possible. We had just been there the year before and were so familiar with all the towns along the coast. Instead, from Junction City, we headed to Eugene then Southeast on Highway 59 to Highway 97, and North to LaPine, Bend and Madras, Maupin and Tygh Valley.

Tygh Valley was recommended to us by our eye doctor in Federal Way, WA. That was the area where he and his friends would hunt for deer every fall. Tygh Valley had one restaurant. There were booths all around the outer walls and a very large round table in the center. The outer tables were where the tourists sat. The round table was where all the locals sat and had their breakfast or morning coffee. We had an incredibly good and large breakfast and enjoyed the conversations of the locals.

From Tygh Valley, we went East and South, visiting Shaniko, Antelope, Fossil, Mitchell and Dayville then on to John Day. From John Day, we went Northeast to Baker City, then West to LaGrande and Pendleton, then along Interstate 84 to Portland, then North on Interstate 5 to Tacoma and home.

Both the Washington and Oregon trips took about a month and were well worth the time spent to learn more about the area of the country that we call home.

And life continues.

CHAPTER 37

Yuma in the Winter
Or
Being Snowbirds

We knew two couples from our association with Kiwanis who wintered in Yuma, Arizona, and they both invited us to come visit on our travels though the Southwest. Our first visit was by car. We stayed at a motel and were there for a week visiting in the homes of our friends and attending a Kiwanis meeting. We didn't see much of the city of Yuma but enjoyed the nice warm weather and some really good home cooked meals and games of cards.

The next year, we drove our motorhome down and stayed in an RV park about 9 miles from our friends' homes. It did not take us long to know that Yuma is a place that we wanted to visit every Winter, so we extended our length of stay every year until we were finally spending a good 6 months there. We lived in our motorhome very comfortably in a 55 and over park. We became involved in park activities and made some very good friends.

In 2018, we bought an older model trailer with 2 bedrooms. The price was right, so we bought it. We painted the complete interior and the exterior. We parked our motorhome in the same spot as usual and Alan's brother came from Colorado and lived in it. For many years, Jim and Alan lived on opposite sides of the country and saw each other for a few days a year if that. It was good for them to have the more consistent contact with each other.

In 2020, for economic reasons, we sold the trailer and went back to living in our Motorhome, but I soon realized that I could not live without an oven and the motorhome only had a convection oven in the microwave. So, we bit the bullet again and bought another park model trailer. It was a little newer and only had one bedroom but had a utility room with a washer and dryer. It did not have an oven though and we had to get creative about putting one in. We finally purchased a wall oven and put it below the stove top.

Activities in the park pretty much shut down during the Pandemic as with everything else. Eventually, they opened up again, but it was not the same. A lot of the winter visitors decided not to return. Alan is back to volunteering once a week at the hospital.

Alan had worked very hard to raise money for the American Legion Post. They badly needed some upgrades in their bar area and needed part of their parking lot paved. He raised enough money to have the upgrades done in the bar.

We have made some very good friends in Yuma but miss our Tacoma friends and family too. In March of 2023, the management of our park decided that they were going to take over the running of all of the activities. We had a social club that planned and executed all of the social activities up until this time. We were not comfortable with the turn of events, so we sold our place and decided to leave the park. Our son Jeff came to Yuma and helped us pack a U-Haul truck and to drive home. After arriving home, Alan decided that driving the motorhome was becoming too much for him and we sold it.

In October, 2023, we rented a trailer in the foothills of Yuma for six weeks, but did not enjoy ourselves as much. When we arrived home the first of December, we decided that we would not go south anymore. We do miss our friends there, but know that we have made the right decision.

Even with age, life does continue.

CHAPTER 38

Jill

Several years ago, Alan's brother Jim gave us DNA test kits. We followed the instructions and sent the kits in. Because we didn't hear anything quickly, I kind of forgot about it. About three months later, Alan received an e-mail indicating that there was a match. All indications showed that he had a daughter.

To back track some: Two weeks before we were married, Alan was at his new job in California, and I was staying at my parents' home. I took a phone call for Alan and whoever was on the other end of the line wanted to know what he was going to do about the baby that was about to be born. After telling him about the call, he did tell me that he fathered a child, but did not know any more than that. That was 51 years ago, and I had forgotten about the call.

Back to the time he found out—I was very upset and hurt. He knew the baby was a girl. She was born a little less than a month after we were married. After she was born and put up for adoption, he sent the mother some money that we did not have to spare.

When I found out about all of this, I was livid. He did not understand why I was so mad. He was so excited and couldn't understand why I wasn't.

Alan talked to her on the phone quite often and learned a little more about her, but I would not stay in the room while he talked to her. I resented those calls. He wanted to meet her as soon as possible. I had said that I did not want to be there. Alan was upset about that and was concerned about how that would make him look. He kept pushing, but I was not giving in until I talked to Emma. We had stopped in Palm Springs to see her on our way home. She made the statement that it was not Jill's fault that she was born and adopted. That statement made me rethink my attitude towards her.

We did stop in Sacramento where she lives. I didn't really want to meet her but felt that I should not be made to leave my home. I did meet her and have grown to like her. She is a sweet lady. We stop to see her every time we go through Sacramento. I have grown to enjoy her company. I accept the fact that Alan has a daughter, but still resent the fact that he did not trust me enough to tell me about her. Our sons were surprised with the news and were reluctant to meet her also. Again, their dad was pushing them to meet her.

As I am writing this, I am sitting in the motorhome parked in an RV Park in Sacramento. We are taking Jill out to dinner this evening and then on Tuesday, she is taking us to Yosemite National Park. Both of us are looking forward to seeing the park.

I have grown to love Jill. She is a lovely lady and we do get along well. This past Summer, we had a Perkins family reunion, and she was able to attend. She met a lot of the family and two of our son's met her. She is now a part of our family.

Even through adversity, life and love continue.

CHAPTER 39

Being Grandparents

Alan and I have seven of the most beautiful, special grandchildren ever. I'm sure every grandparent feels that way about their grandchildren, but ours really are the most special. Six of them are adults now and the other one is well on her way. Three of the girls are married and we have two great-granddaughters and one more on the way.

The strongest advice I could give any of these incredible individuals is to not let everyday life get in the way of enjoying and loving your partner. Don't just exist, but live. My hope in writing this is that they will maintain a knowledge and history of their paternal grandmother's side of the family.

Life does indeed continue.

CHAPTER 40

Three of our seven grandchildren are married. All three of them had totally different types of weddings. Michaela is married to Alex and was married in his mother's back yard in a simple ceremony with Alex's mother officiating. Michaela wore a long dress with small blue flowers on a white background. She absolutely glowed with happiness.

Susie is married to Jeremy. They were married just before Christmas last year. They went to the courthouse and had a very simple, direct ceremony with only their witnesses there.

Emma was married to Logan in a formal wedding in her in-law's back yard, wearing a long white dress, a veil, and Birkenstocks. She was going to be comfortable. There were about 80 people there and a formal dinner was served after the ceremony. It was a magical wedding and just what Emma wanted. In fact, all three of the weddings were just what the bride and groom wanted.

We look forward to more of our grandchildren finding their life partners and we look forward to more great-grandchildren. Who could ask for more?

With much love and joy, life continues.

EPILOGUE

The Stuart Women

Mary Jane Stuart

Margaret, Gramma Startin, Alice Simmons, Mary Jane Stuart

Margaret, Mary Jane, Alice, Mary Alice

The previous writings are some of my remembrances of stories told to me by members of my family and actual events that I was involved in. It has been enlightening remembering all of this. The stories told to me give me such sweet memories. he events I was personally involved in are so vivid. As I was writing about a certain subject, another story would pop up in my memory. I had lists of ideas to write about.

My hope is that my children and grandchildren will read this and gain some insight into this incredible family and its history. I believe that everyone should know where they come from and about the people that have shaped their lives. With birth, death, marriage and divorce, a family changes. When I was born, there were five generations of women living, as there were when my mother was born. I had a great-great grandmother, two great-grandmothers, two grandmothers, a grandfather, a mother, a father, and a brother. My Mother was an only child, and my father had a brother and a sister. The family I was close to where my great-aunts and great grandmothers. I had the privilege of knowing them very well.

LIFE AND LOVE CONTINUE

The Stuart Sisters, their mother and Grandmother lived long, hard lives well into their 80's. Except for great-great-great grandma Startin and great-great grandma Stuart, three of the four sisters had more than one marriage. Divorce was not common then, but three of them were divorced. All four of them worked at jobs outside their homes and three of them were raising their children at the same time, with no husband to help them.

None of the sisters ever owned a home. They either rented or lived with a relative, yet they were all happy ladies to be around and would do almost anything for their friends and family.

I had the privilege of knowing all four of the sisters plus their brother, Uncle IO. He was also a very special man and in their later years, he rode herd on them.

None of the sisters were overly religious, but all had a deep belief in a higher power and respected the right of everyone to believe as they wished. It has been very enlightening remembering all this. They were strong and independent women, sincere in their beliefs and ready for anything. The stories told to me by my grandma's relatives give me strength.

When I was little, it was always fun to visit them. I got lots of attention and special treats.

As I am sitting here writing this, I am remembering specific visits to each of them. At Aunt Stella's we wandered around her farm and picked berries that would be made into jams and jellies. At Aunt Minnie's, we had tea parties with little cakes and cookies and special tea for me. She even had a small teacup.

At Nano's, I sat and listened to her stories about the Indians who rode on the boat with her and how she cooked special meals for them.

Aunt Dede was my mentor. I would stop to visit her when I was feeling down and depressed, usually about my love life, or lack thereof. She would always cheer me up. I did not know her when I was little. I was in my 20's when she became my very good friend. She was independent and sincere in her beliefs and was ready for almost anything.

God has been exceedingly good to me throughout my 80 some years. I had ancestors who were strong, but loving people who took risks and shaped the family into what we are today. I had grandparents who were willing to take care of me when I needed them. I had a mother, who for 60 years, loved and nurtured me and gave me a solid foundation to build from. I had a father who, even though we were not close, shaped me in his own way. I had a stepfather, along with his family who became my family and gave me love and encouragement. I had a brother who loved me unconditionally and gave me constant encouragement. I had a stepbrother who became my brother very quickly after his father and my mother married. He was always there when I needed him. I have three sons, three daughters-in-law, along with seven grandchildren who are the lights of my life. And, I have a husband who is my rock!

Life and Love have continued as they should have.

ACKNOWLEDGEMENTS

I have a strong feeling that my family, especially the Stuart's have been telling me to write their story. There are so many people to thank besides my ancestors for their continued encouragement and contributions to this book. Thank you to my sons and daughters-in-law for their encouragement, enthusiasm, and excitement. To my grandson Christopher, who spent hours at my computer making sure that the table-of-contents made some sense and putting the book together. Special thanks to Jeff. He is a marvel at figuring out my computer and helping straighten out my messes. And to Patrick for his very valued advice, his computer skills, and his frequent trips to the post office for me. And to Steven for his constant encouragement, love, and his outstanding grilling skills. He and Shareen have fed us well. I do treasure you all.

Special thanks to friend Fran, who read the first few pages of this book and gave me the encouragement I needed to continue. Also, thanks to friend Karen for editing part of the book for me. Her advice was very much appreciated.

Thanks to all my grandchildren for being excited to read the book. It is their history.

And to Alan, my husband of 55 years who has given me nothing but encouragement and love throughout this project.

Parts of the book were hard to write and might be hard for some of my family to read, but they are a part of my life and memories. I can't write about the good without including the bad. Fortunately, there have been more good than bad and I am eternally grateful.

I miss the family that are gone and dearly love and treasure the ones still in my life.

All the stories and memories prove that life does continue and with love included, can be very good.

JUDITH COTTINGHAM PERKINS

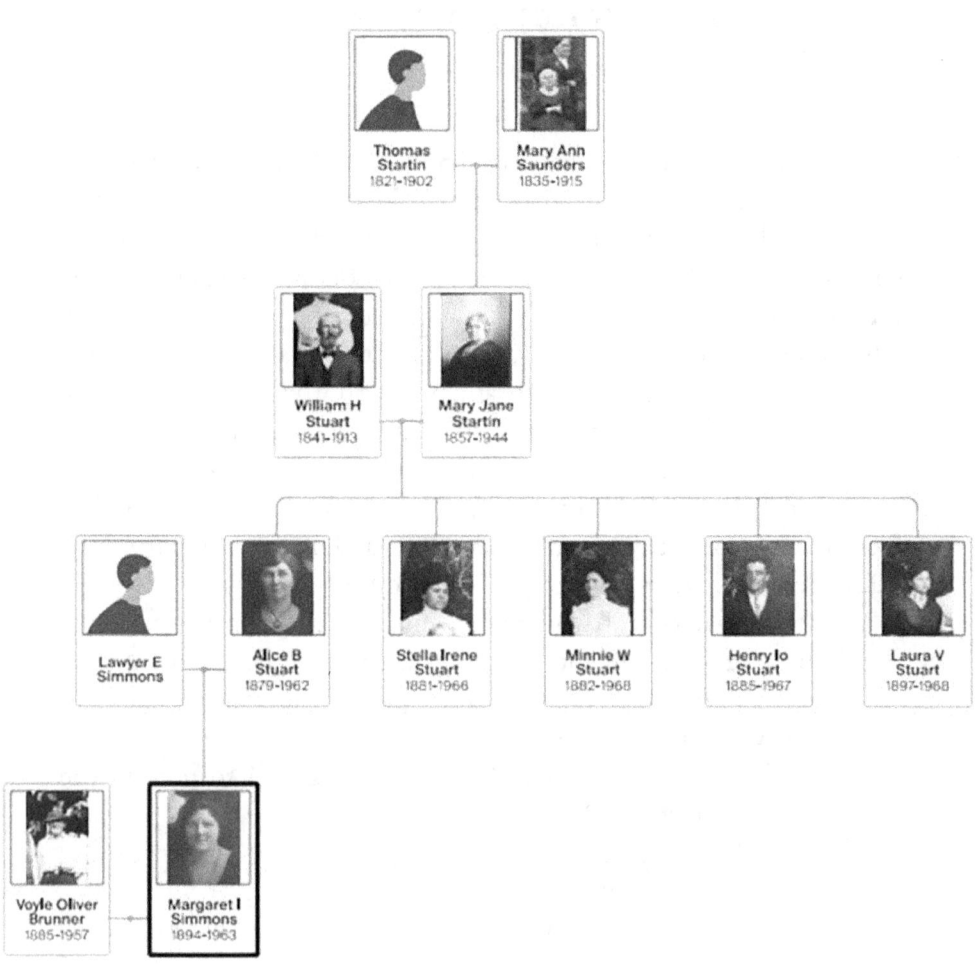

LIFE AND LOVE CONTINUE

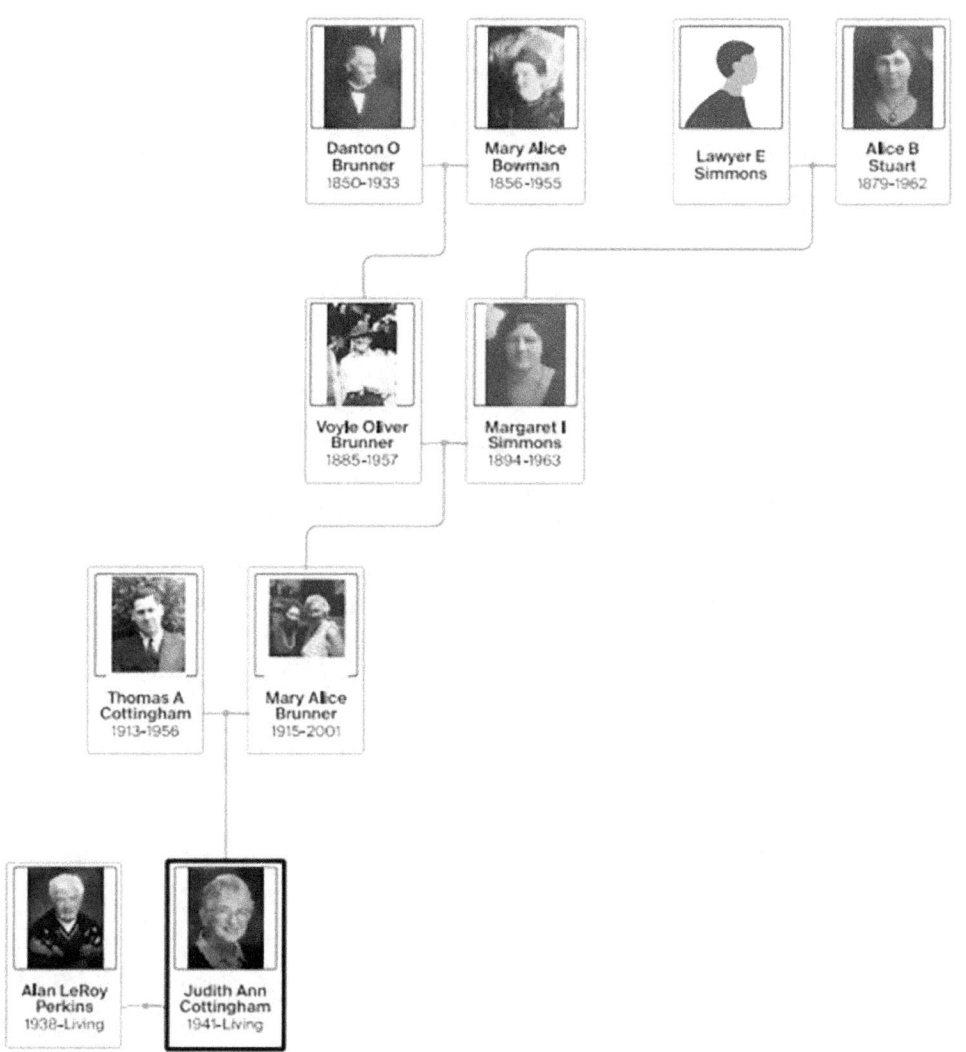

PICTURES

Danton Oliver Brunner

Mary Alice Brunner - 90 years' old

Alice Blanche Stuart

Voyle O. Brunner

Margaret Simmons

Voyle and Mary Alice

Tom and Mary Alice

Margaret Brunner

Tom Cottingham

Estella Mitchell Cottingham

LIFE AND LOVE CONTINUE

Danny and
Judy- 1944

Multnomah
falls picnic

Dan Cottingham

Dan Cottingham and
Mary Alice Talbott

Aunt Dede

John and Bob Talbott

John Talbott

John, Mary Alice Talbott and Steven Perkins

Alan Perkins

Judith Cottingham Perkins

Judith and Alan Perkins Wedding

LIFE AND LOVE CONTINUE

Mary Jane Stuart   Margaret, Gramma Startin, Alice Simmons, Mary Jane

Margaret, Mary Jane, Alice, Mary Alice   William Henry Stuart

The Red House   Scow on Snake River at Riperia

The Depot at Riperia

FROM THIS

5 generations - 1941

5 generations – 1915   5 generations - 1942

TO THIS

The Alan Perkins family - 2013

www.ingramcontent.com/pod-product-compliance
Lightning Source LLC
LaVergne TN
LVHW021823060526
838201LV00058B/3494